BROKEN DREAMS

Broken Pieces Series

~ Book 3 ~

MARTHA PEREZ

BROKEN DREAMS

For more information or to book an event, please email
the following:

Martha Perez - memartha@ymail.com

Sal Andalon - salandalon@ymail.com

Or visit www.marthaperez.info

Edited by Dr. Vonda at FirstEditing.com

Cover design and print format by The Book Khaleesi
www.thebookkhaleesi.com

Self-Published in 2017 by Sal Andalon

ISBN-10: 0-692-88153-0
ISBN-13: 978-0-692-88153-8

PRINTED IN THE UNITED STATES OF AMERICA

10 9 8 7 6 5 4 3 2 1

DEDICATION

Writing this story about Josh and Emily's life was great. I sincerely hope you enjoy this story as much as I loved writing it.

I want to take this opportunity to thank my husband Sal for encouraging and loving me to write this story.

Special thanks to my daughter Patricia and my son Rudy and my two granddaughters: love you.

PROLOGUE

Josh

It was a sunny beautiful day. I remember way back when I was ten and we moved to a three-bedroom house next to an awesome park called Montecito Heights in the mid-60s. We were excited, Mom and Dad, Kyle and me, and my little sister Debbie. Life was good back then, no worries, very young and carefree. We were good kids.

And then the unthinkable happened three years later my brother died. A drunk driver ran over him while he was walking from the market. I never got over him leaving me. We were best buddies, best friends, brothers.

My girlfriend's name was Abigail Marie Pena. She was my beautiful Abby. My name is Josh Maxwell. I was in love with Abby but chose my path in life drinking, doing drugs and fucking different women.

Trevor McQueen is my best friend–well, he was Rick's best friend first until he slept with Betty Cox. Well, we slept with Betty; she was our dream girl. She was in love with sex. Trevor and I would share girls in high school. We did drugs together, then I got married to that pest of a girl that I hated, Emily Johnson, the mean girl in school. She hurt Abby with her best friend Betty.

I recollect when I met Abby walking into class, a girl with short dark hair like someone butchered her hair in anger. She seemed embarrassed, dropping her pencil. I picked it up for her, telling her she had butterfingers, and her cheeks got all rosy. She didn't talk much but she blushed a lot. Her hazel eyes were cheerless but absolutely beautiful.

I could hear Betty and Emily making fun of her, the bullies. My whole body tensed. I wanted shut them up; after all, we were only ten years old. I was Abby best friend. She had a best friend once; his name was Rick Owen. He was jealous of me but I didn't care much! Rick was hanging with the mean girls in school, hurting Abby.

Things changed after Kyle died. I thought I had to let her go. Abby was my girlfriend in middle school. I never wanted to hurt Abby. When I let her go I never looked back, then my life became worthless with drinking, drugs and so many girls and women…

Will I ever change my life? I don't think so, not for anyone. I'm a cocky bastard. I do whatever I want and no person will ever tell me otherwise. I don't want to be saved. I love my life the way it is, with drugs, lust and nasty sex. My poor mom tried to change me. Guess what? She couldn't succeed. I really felt bad for her.

Dad just said, "He's still a young boy; leave him alone." Being grateful was an understatement. Dad didn't care what I did anymore, and that was fine with me.

CHAPTER 1

Josh

When my brother died I just changed for the worse. Kyle was my best friend, my brother, and he's gone. He loved Megan, Abby's sister. We were in love with sisters when the storm came into my young life. That horrific rainy night the night changed our happy lives forever. My family was broken. Our dreams vanished from our hearts and souls. I cried so much for my brother. I still remember the day. I went to school to tell Abby I wasn't good for her and when I said goodbye, holding her so tight, whispering in her ear that I would always care for her, what she didn't know is I loved her with all my heart. It takes a real young man to let someone you love go. Her tears rolling down her sweet cheeks as she whispered in my ear, "I don't want you to let me go." I broke her heart, saying to myself it was for the best. I was angry and destructive to myself and whoever came along for the ride.

A few days passed in school, and Abby saw me with Emily. I was kissing her, feeling her breasts, making hickeys all over her neck. She was so willing, and I took advantage of what came to me. My heart stopped when I saw Abby was watching us. I pushed Emily away from me, running quickly to Abby. "Sorry you saw that."

"It's none of my business you; let me go, Josh!" My heart was aching for her. What Abby didn't know was she touched all of our lives. I am that guy who, when I let go, I don't look back ever. I don't cry for any chick, not even Abby. It doesn't mean I didn't miss her; truth be told, I'm a fuck-up, dude.

Years passed we're in high school Emily was persistent like a tick in embedded in your skin or a puppy following me everywhere. Emily always gave me a sour taste in my mouth. She is a pretty girl; don't get me wrong. She has light brown eyes, long dark hair, tan skin, a curvaceous body and a small waist. Her breasts are larger than my hand. To me she was like any other girl.

Trevor is having a party and everyone will be there. I go to his house to party. The music playing and everyone is having fun. It's very loud when I walk in. I check out the scene to see what girl to fuck my brains. I scoped out my surroundings. Rick the prick is kissing Betty. Trevor gives me a beer. I really needed something stronger than a fucking beer. My mood is craving something, maybe some drugs, that will make me fuck all night. Let me find a participant. The party is rocking Trevor and I go to the restroom to do some white powder, up our nose. I'm feeling fantastic and horny so I look for my prey while staring at Rick devour Betty.

Gossip all over school is she took his virginity. She's a nasty whore. My virginity was lost after Kyle died. Years later I went with an older woman who taught me everything I needed to know. She liked sucking my cock a lot; of course, a young buck like me loved the training for free. I'm a cocky bastard who doesn't have any feelings for anyone but myself.

Emily

Walking into the party I see him, the one who stole my heart. All my thoughts of him are so naughty. I can't wait to jump his bones. Josh Maxwell always pushes me away, but not tonight. I'm going sleep with him. I'm not a virgin, so he won't have a problem. Wishing tonight will be with him is all my heart and body desires. I get so hot and bothered just thinking about his hands all over me, his lips sucking my bottom lip… He's always in my dreams. His bluish-gray eyes haunt my dreams. I always wanted to run my fingers through his jet black hair. Ever since seeing him I wanted him, but he was always with Abby. Josh hated me for hurting Abby. He didn't understand how jealous I was of her. She was so plain. Rick and Josh were all over her all the time. I didn't understand; she was a simple girl. I've changed; I'm not that mean girl anymore. Anyway Abby vanished and Betty was ecstatic; now she was all over Rick. She has him around her finger-- she tells him to jump, he jumps. I look around. The music is getting louder. A sweet, good-looking guy gives me a drink. Taking it to take the edge off, I sway my hips to the music, staring at Josh dancing with a slut and looking away because I hate anyone touching him.

Trevor's voice whispers in my ear, "You want to dance, baby girl?" I stare at him. He's gorgeous, with green eyes, fair skin and his dark brown hair pulled back. He is muscular, wearing a black t-shirt and a pair of fitted jeans. What girl would say no! So I give a sweet smile at him and we go dance. Feeling eyes on me, I turn around. Josh stares at me and I give him a cheeky smile, hoping he'll come to me. A girl can wish, right? Betty always told me, "Watch out what you wish for; it might be the biggest mistake in your life."

Trevor is dancing so close to me I can feel his warm breath on my neck. "Listen honey, do you want to come to my place? My mom went Fresno for the weekend."

"Why would I do that?"

"Because we could have a party, just you and me."

He gives me mischievous grin.

My head turns to Josh. He's kissing that slut. Being so jealous, I turn back, smiling at Trevor. "Sure, let's party. It will be just us, right?"

"You better believe it, baby girl."

We drive to his house. Trevor touches my hand

and I feel electricity all the way down my spine and wetness between my legs. He licks his full lips and my nipples harden. Trevor parks his car and opens my door for me. What a gentleman--guys will do whatever just to get laid.

"Come on, Emily, my room has all the works!" We run upstairs. He opens the bedroom door. I am

surprised. It's extremely clean; he even has a miniature refrigerator. Of course, he has a blue comforter, huge pillows and a small bathroom.

"Would you like a drink, Emily?"

"Sure!"

"Do you like sex, baby girl?"

Boy, that was an unexpected question. "Yes!"

We're drinking our beer. "Do you trust me?"

"I guess."

He gives me a pill. "You're going to have so many orgasms, baby girl."

I wanted to roll my eyes. I swallowed it down with my beer and almost choked. Trevor watches me. Half an hour later I was a little relaxed--more like very relaxed. He put some music on to smooth the mood. Trevor wasn't kidding; I was getting hot!

"Are you relaxed yet, Emily?"

Nodding is all I could manage. His mischievous smile was gorgeous.

I expected him to be rough with me, or at least brutal at some point to have his way with me--that's what I heard from gossip at school. He surprised me by teasing me with his finger, sliding so softly, tracing my face to my neck, pinching my nipples. He's a teaser and a very smooth one at that. I was feeling a sensation I never felt before.

"Listen honey, I will devour you completely. You're going to feel what a real man feels like." Even though he's in his teens, he's making me so wet with those words. "Do you tell all the girls that?"

"You want to feel my cock, girl? It's huge even for your soft, tight little sweet pussy. My cock will make you beg for more!"

I want to laugh but I don't because guys like him will get angry. I put my hand on his bulge. Oh my God; it's huge! He grins. We are going slowly. He removes my blouse at a snail's pace. I'm wearing my new pink lace bra. He smells my hair and kisses my lips; his tongue is long and thick. All I could think was what kind of sensation he could do to my pussy, not to mention his huge cock; it's probably phenomenal. Thinking about it is making me hot and wet. I've only been with guys that are drunk out of their asses. My first time he hurt me and came fast. Trevor is taking me out of my thoughts.

"Stop thinking, baby girl." He removes my bra and backs up to watch me. "Hmmm! You're beautiful, Emily."

I smile. He's complimenting me; that's a first. No guy ever takes the time to say much.

"Emily, lie on the bed and spread your legs, baby girl." Trevor pulls my g-string with his teeth and starts to lick my leg. Oh my God! He's teasing me out of my mind; I can't even think. "Emily, you will never forget the way I fuck you; that's a promise."

He was the best fuck I ever had so far and I welcomed with so much anticipation. It was like my body sparkled with fire and lust. At that moment I wanted him to fuck me to show he wanted me too! Our hormones were in overdrive.

Emily

He starts licking my sweet spot with that huge, long tongue of his, and the feeling was astonishing. I kept squirming. "Stay still, girl." My intense orgasm came full force; he devoured all my essence. Trevor was relentless, licking my pussy clean, and then he started to consume me with his hot breath, biting my breasts putting his tongue in my naval, rubbing his steel pipe of a cock. "Ready for me, baby girl?" I was speechless.

He gave me a cocky grin as he slid his huge, long dick in. I was little uncomfortable at first but I was adjusting quickly and was anxious to feel him. The intense sensation was phenomenal.

"Yeah! Oh! Yeah! Ahhhh!" I squeezed the life out of his muscular arms. The sounds that were coming out of my mouth were "Fuck! Yea!" Both of our sweaty bodies slapped together as we pounded each other with need and lust and so much passion. This was my first experience having amazing orgasms. Trevor kissed my lips sweetly. I grabbed his hair firmly with our body-hugging.

"The night is still young, baby girl. You rest; you will need me for some more." I was getting wet just listening to him talking.

My heart will always be with Josh. Why I can't like Trevor? That would've made life simpler, but my life is never effortless. Trevor is very kind. It surprised me a great deal, almost like he wanted me for a while. That's me just over-thinking things. All I ever wanted was Josh. Love is blind in so many ways. Your heart chooses a heart that maybe won't want love you back. Trevor's body is warm and sweaty and most of all inviting, holding me softly, his large hands wrapped around me, letting me stay in his arms. What a shock! But it's nice cuddling closer to him as he holds me tighter. How sweet to be comforted. I always yearned for someone to hold me just because. I will hold this feeling for a long time. I take a deep breath to enjoy his cologne; it smells wonderful. I close my eyes and fall asleep with no care in the world but with the wrong guy. He's just not Josh.

CHAPTER 2

Trevor

What was I thinking? Emily is sleeping in my arms when she likes Josh. This isn't me at all. I just like having sex with girls, and here I'm holding her. I never let them stay over. What could I have

possibly been thinking? I act different with her. I'm the bad boy in high school. Josh and I are too young for this shit. Our bodies are close-fitting, like she belongs in my arms. I don't want to fall in love with a girl who cares for another guy. Thinking of last night, I love feeling her smooth skin and the sounds she made she were making me weak. I wanted to be forceful with her but I just couldn't. What am I, a wimp? Now my pipe is getting hard again. What the fuck is going on?

She starts, stirs and my lips hit roughly on her swollen lips. I bite firmly on her bottom lip. She moans with our morning breath. My cock starts to grow like a snake that wants to eat the kill. She starts to feel me. "Get on top of me, baby girl, and show me what you got!"

My length disappears inside her sweet spot. As she slowly sat down on my huge cock, it was a moment of purest satisfaction and we shuddered with bliss in each other arms. We stay like that for a while, then reality kicks in and I take her home.

I go see Josh; of course he has a hangover. "Did you bang that chick, Trevor?"

"Say her name, Josh; her name is Emily."

"I know her name, Trevor; don't forget I sucked her breasts in junior high. She has pink nipples for that tan skin of hers."

"You're an asshole, Josh."

"Yeah, an asshole that Emily wishes to fuck!"

"Look dude, I banged her."

"That's ok, Trevor; you're just marinating her for me, or we both could fuck her together."

"NO! It was just a one-time thing; go get her if you want her."

"I will, all in good time, my friend; don't worry. I'll tell you every detail." He grinned sarcastically.

All I could do is shake my head. *He is truly a number one asshole,* I thought. I was bad but he takes the whole cake. Thinking about Emily, I try to take my thoughts somewhere else. She's not mine. At least I got to taste that sweet pussy. Sometimes it's not good to fuck the wrong girl because you can't have what you want. Sometimes life sucks. Her heart belongs to Josh and he will never love her, never.

Josh

Getting ready to go party, I heard Emily is going to be there. Now is my chance to get Trevor jealous. Trevor is honking and I rush to his dad's station wagon. Yeah! We looked like dumbasses. If it wasn't for our looks we would look like nerds; in that pathetic car we're just chumps. We could hear the music thumping. We started drinking on the way over there.

"Fuck! Trevor, did you spray Old English from your dad? You stink!"

"Shut up asshole, got to smell good for the chicks." We chuckle. "What about you? You smell like Brut; that stinks worse."

We look around at all the fine chicks in Alex's house. He comes toward Trevor and me with a couple of cold beers, then we go to his bedroom. He had some white powder. We put the coke up our nose and we're ready to party and whatever comes next.

Scoping the room, I saw Emily was here, so I could get her in the sack. I could see Trevor watching her. He really liked her for some reason. I'm going to fuck her tonight, to see what all the fuss is about. I walk to Emily. She seems surprised. I can't blame the poor girl. I'm going to have fun with her. I fuck them and leave them; that's the game. She's smiling like she won the award; it's comical really. Dancing slowly, I start to hold her plump ass. She smells like candy.

She starts to turn to Trevor. He turns quickly, so I squeeze her ass tighter. "Let's go out back." She nods. Trevor gets a girl and he leaves the party. Poor guy, he takes the fun out of everything. Taking two beers for us, we're in the backyard. Emily licks her lips. "Come here, Emmy."

She walks slowly to me and I stick my tongue down her throat. Her sounds are making my junk get larger by the minute. "Feel my cock throb, Emmy?"

"Yes," she says with a low voice.

That's all I needed to hear. "Let's get the hell out of here." My broad, mischievous smile gets huge.

Getting girls to follow me is easy; they are extremely predictable easy sluts. It's easy to get pussy and easier to get drugs. I do it more to numb my aching heart. Kyle would be disappointed for my sad existence but it is what it is. My life will never change.

Josh & Emily

I take her to a motel. She's drinking her beer. I'm taking my black t-shirt off. I get next to her, taking hold of her hair, making her look at my grayish-blue eyes. "Listen Emmy, I'm going to fuck you hard. My appetite is huge, if you know what I mean?"

"So what do you want from me, Josh?"

"What do you think? Your pussy, that's what! I'm not Trevor that's all nice; I always want hardcore sex and pussy."

"Well, come and get it then."

I go to her tearing her blouse; her buttons fall in the floor. She's wearing a black bra that has white hearts. I grab her hair once again, sucking her neck with my tongue, making marks.

"That's all you got, Josh?"

That's when I lift her up and push her against the wall. "Put your arm over your head." I suck her breast roughly. Rubbing her vagina, my two fingers go inside.

"Oh! Josh, yeah!"

"You like it rough, Emily?" I lift her up and throw her on the bed. "Get on your knees. The thought of your mouth wrapping around my pulsating rod is driving me insane. Get on the edge of the bed toward me and suck my thick pole. It needs the mouth of a slut like you to suck it hard so I can fuck that hot, tight pussy of yours."

She didn't waste any time removing my jeans. She

stares at my cock. "It's huge and thick for you but I'll make it fit." She is staring at me. "Like what you see, Emmy?" I take a hold of my huge pole. She licks her lips. "Don't hold back when you suck this big stick." I shove my cock in her mouth. She gags at first. I know she's sexually aroused, the way I treat her. Fuck, Emmy's mouth has a firm grip of my massive cock. "Aaahh! That feels good." I stop her and lay her on the bed. "Spread your thighs." I suck, lick and devour her clit. Damn, she tastes like sweet candy. She is so obedient. "Is your wet pussy throbbing yet?" Her sweet juices are dripping out of her tight cunt. The more insulting I get, the hotter she gets. She screams with her orgasm. I grab her hips and shove my dick way inside, not wasting anytime. Her dripping wet pussy gushes down with my cum. I didn't use a condom--fuck!

Emily sure liked my aggressive behavior toward her. I kind of feel sorry for her but this is what she wanted for a long time. After we finish fucking I just straight out tell her, "Get up. I'm taking you home."

"Why, Josh?"

"Because you got what you wanted, Emmy--my cock."

I could see tears flowing down her flushed cheeks.

"You think I give a shit? Well, I don't, so hurry up!"

"You tore my blouse."

"Put my t-shirt and I'll take you home."

After taking Emily home I go to Trevor's house. He's drinking by himself. He throws me a beer. "Where is your shirt?"

"I tore her blouse."

"So did you bang her?"

"Sure did! She had a tight pussy but you already know that."

"You don't have to talk about her that way, Josh."

"What's wrong, jealous dude?"

"I'm not! Just don't talk about her that way; she not

like the other girls we fuck, Josh."

"Whatever. To me she is another quest under my belt."

We drink the night away, smoking pot and talking about nothing important. In back of my mind I was worried about not using protection when I fucked Emily. With my luck she'll get pregnant. Why am I frustrated about this shit? I pull my jet black hair with my fingers. Being in Trevor room I couldn't even sleep; the fucker snores loud. I leave for my house. It's always silent ever since Kyle passed. I hate this house now. It's not the same anymore. I pop some sleeping pills and sleep like a stone.

"Josh, wake up so you can eat some breakfast."

"Not hungry, Mom!"

"You always say that. Get up and let's eat like a family."

I put my pillow over my head. "I don't want to hear it, Mom."

She walks out, probably upset. I feel badly about it

but she knows not to come to my room. I'm just an asshole.

CHAPTER 3

Emily

It is a beautiful sunny day and the worst day of my life. I just found out I'm two months pregnant. I'm feeling nauseous, moody and sobbing and to make matters worse, I haven't seen Josh or Trevor. Being depressed, I call Betty, telling her what's going on.

"Are you sure, Emmy?"

"Yes, I am sure."

"You have to tell Josh."

"For what? So he could say it's not his? And to top it off I have to tell my mother and my dad. They're going to kill me, Betts. I'm only seventeen. I only have a year to go for high school. I had dreams, you know. Talk to you later. Mom is home; got to break the bad news."

"Ok girl, good luck."

"Thanks Betty."

I walk to the kitchen. "Hi Emily, help me with groceries."

"Okay mother, can we talk?"

"Sure sweetheart, what is it?"

"I really think you're going to be mad at me." My tears slip down my face.

"What's wrong Emmy?"

I spit it out so fast, "I'm having a baby."

"Are you serious? You're having sex already? Why Emily? How could you be so careless? What are you going to do? And who's the father?"

"It's Josh."

"Well, he better marry you. Go to your room. I can't be in the same room with you right now."

I run to my room sobbing. My mother never speaks to me that way. I hurt her; who could blame her? She's disappointed in me. When my dad found out it was the worst day of my life. We cried. He had dreams for me, just like every other parents. I wanted to go to college to be a lawyer. Now I'm having a baby. Now I'm becoming a mother, and it is Josh's baby. I call Trevor to tell Josh I need to talk to him, hanging up quickly. He never called me; he was getting ready to go to a party at some friend's house, of course, touching some slut's ass. It hurt my heart. He doesn't care about me. Breathing deeply, what I'm about to do is push the slut. She falls to the floor.

"What the fuck is wrong with you, Emily?

"Listen Josh, I'm having your baby!"

Everyone went silent.

"How do you know it's mine? You sleep around. You fucked Trevor."

"Oh my God! Josh, you're so fucked up! It's yours! My mom and dad want to talk to you next Friday for dinner; be there." I leave so fast with tears in my eyes. What could I expect from a broken guy? Maybe one day I could save him. I love him so much. I hope one day he will love me back.

Emily

As I'm getting my books for class, Trevor gives me an apple. Rolling my eyes, I ask, "What do you want?"

"I'm just trying to be nice, Emmy. I do care about you."

"Yeah, right. Just leave me alone."

He smirks. "Why are you mean to me?"

"Just leave."

"Whatever you say. You're acting like a bitch right now."

"No one asked for your option, Trevor. You're just as bad as your best friend Josh."

"He will never love you, Emily He will hurt you and destroy you."

"What, you're my daddy now?"

"I'm just warning you, the dude doesn't care about anyone. Do you want to suffer? If you make him love you, Emmy, he will make you miserable! What do I care?" Trevor, with a sad and angry face, leaves and slams the locker, and I run to my next class.

I'm home once again and call my best friend Betty and tell her what Josh and Trevor said. Betty always has an answer. "Fuck them. Just have your baby and go on. I have a date, Emmy."

"With who?"

"This time some guy I met from school."

"Okay, have fun, Betts."

"I always do, Emmy. Take care."

I stare at the ceiling, holding my tummy and talking to the baby. I will always love my little munchkin. I go to my English class. Josh is messing around with some girl, sticking his fingers up her skirt.

I run to the girls' restroom to vomit because I'm so dusted. One the girls asks if I'm feeling okay. My tears of hurt sliding down my face, I tell her I'm just feeling a little under the weather. She nods walks out. I stay, standing like a weak girl that a guy doesn't want, just a walking disaster.

The rest of the day was long. Going home, I am walking slowly. Mom has dinner for me. Smiling at her motherly love, I only wish to be a great mom too.

Betty calls me. "That guy was so yummy."

"I thought you were with Rick."

"I am, silly; my sex drive is huge. When you fuck different guys, it's so exciting. Emmy, too bad you're having a baby; you needed to explore more."

"Thanks Betts, you always make me feel good."

Friday Josh is meeting my mom and dad. I'm the only child. Of course, Josh comes late. My dad is totally angry. Mom made fried chicken, rice and salad. Josh looks so cute, his short jet-black hair pulled back, some jeans, a pullover long sleeve shirt--he has always been gorgeous. Dad wakes me up from my thoughts.

"So Josh, what are your intentions for my daughter?"

"Well sir, I could marry her."

"Good. Finish your dinner. This will happen two weeks from today. We are going to Vegas. Invite a few friends".

Two weeks pass quickly. All our families are in Vegas, along with my friend Betty and Rick and, of course, Trevor.

Josh & Emily

"Stop moving, sweetheart!"

"I'm nervous, Mom."

"I know, dear. Just stay still. This is your big day. Let me put your last pin in your hair. That dress is beautiful."

My white satin dress is short. My heels are a bit high. My hair is up, sexy strands flowing down my face.

Betty walks in my room "Wow! You are beautiful."

I really wanted to roll my eyes. She's the one who's always lovely. All the guys want her so badly. She sleeps around like she changes underwear. I hate the way Josh always stares at her. Long blonde silky hair, a perfect body, green eyes sparkling at every guy in sight--I've been so jealous of her since grammar school, when we were the mean girls.

We drive to the chapel just hoping an Elvis impersonator doesn't marry us, because that would be an embarrassment to me. Everyone is standing and staring at me. When I see Josh he takes my breath away. He is wearing a black suit, his jet-black hair gelled and pulled back, even though his gray-blue eyes don't shine like a man in love Trevor stares at me like he wants to tell me something. My life sucks. Trevor is the best man and Betty is my maid of honor. Josh is staring at her with a grin like *I'm going to fuck you later, after the ceremony.*

We all go to a buffet. Josh is drinking a great deal. My dad tells him to stop drinking. "It is your honeymoon."

He drinks a large amount more. My stomach starts to ache. "I'm going to our hotel room."

Josh follows me. "Emmy, you're going to bed already?"

"Josh, you could stay with me."

"I'm in Vegas. Go to sleep. You're a boring bitch." He slams the door. My tears slide down my face. So it begins, the beginning to an end. He doesn't love me.

What did I expect from him, just to run in my arms with a blissful kiss? I fall asleep.

Josh comes to the room at five in morning. He smells of sex and perfume. He stumbles to the bed, trying to touch me.

"Don't touch me."

He says, "Okay!"

That's all that was said between us. Josh wakes up early, takes a shower and gets back in bed. "Come wife, let me fuck you, Emmy."

"I don't think so! Josh, you probably fucked every girl you saw last night."

He smirks. "And if I did, Trevor joined me."

He laughs at my face. Why he would do this to me is beyond me; all I ever did was love him, heart and soul. I run to the restroom and vomit my guts out, with tears of hurt and such sadness. Wiping my mouth with a towel, I finish putting on my black short skirt and white sweater and go to eat by myself.

CHAPTER 4

Trevor

I couldn't believe Josh left Emily in the hotel on their wedding night. He went with me to some strip bar. We started to drink, watching all the fine women swaying their naked bodies, and what happened next was lots of sex. We had an orgy with two women in my hotel room. I had a blonde with huge breasts and a nice figure. Josh's woman had dark brown hair. She had small tits but a huge ass. We went to the bedroom. The two chicks couldn't wait for us young bucks. I had my fair of orgies, but they were girls from high school. Josh doesn't waste any time; he pulled her hair. She gasps. The blonde and I stare at them. We are drunk and horny so we join in with the foreplay, sharing the blonde and brunette, kissing, licking, slurping each other--we were a tangled mess. I don't know how Josh got the blonde but he sucks her large melons rough and he spanks the other chick's huge ass. She giggles. Their pussies were so soaked. It made my cock stir to life. We were all fucking and banging each other. Good thing we had condoms, a huge box. We took turns fucking; we had a blast.

When I woke up the next day felt a little guilty participating with Josh in escapades of lust. Josh and I are similar in so many ways; the difference is I have heart and Josh doesn't. I took a shower. The room smells like nasty sex mixed with alcohol. Josh is still wrapped up with the two chicks; no doubt he'll fuck them both himself.

"Hey sugar, come join us, baby." Her tits showing

were making my cock stir to life again. I was thinking of Emily. It's Josh that should go after her. "Come on, baby."

I couldn't disappoint her. I remove my clothes. "Let's go to the restroom.

"Sure sugar, I don't mind taking a shower with you and that huge cock of yours." She smiles. "I'm going to make you scream my name."

I could hear Josh having sex with the brunette; all that noise she's making got me horny. We're in the shower. The water is flowing on Blondie's body. Her melons were in my face. My tongue licks and caresses. She gets on her knees and grips my huge, long cock and begins to suck so rough. My cum explodes in her mouth; my cum is dripping from her mouth. I help her up. "Turn around and bend a little." She does what I say; that's what's good about older women—they're very experienced. My cock comes to life again. I'm rubbing my cock in her backside and she moans. I slammed her and her screams were earsplitting with our climax and the feeling of pleasure.

Josh leaves at five in the morning and the chicks leave after I go back to sleep. I'm single and entitled to do whatever I want. I can't even move my legs from all that nasty sex I had.

Emily

Having morning sickness didn't help the way I'm feeling. Nauseated, sitting by myself in one of those buffets, I must look pathetic. I probably shouldn't eat. My stomach is upset, like someone is doing cartwheels. I have so many regrets. I haven't even had my baby yet. What about Josh? He's shameless, trying sleep with me without taking a shower--so gross.

Mom wakes me up out of my thoughts. "Hi honey, how was your honeymoon? Where's Josh?" "Sleeping." No way I was telling my mom my husband slept with who knows who!

"Let's eat, honey."

"Sure mom."

We went shopping and walking around. We're going home tomorrow. I went back to the room. Josh wasn't there. Well, that figures. Will we ever be on the same page? I'm watching television with a pout when there's a knock. Opening the door, I roll my eyes. "What do you want?"

"Just checking to see if you're ok."

"I'm fine!"

"Why are you here by yourself?"

"Look, I'm not feeling good right now, so leave!"

"Why do you treat me like this?"

"Like what Trevor, the asshole you are? You're the one who takes Josh to every girl you see." "Don't blame me for what he does. Let me remind you that this is what's going on around you. It will happen all the time."

"No help from you, right; you can't have sex

without him or what?"

"I can see you're agitated."

"I'm more irritated."

"Obviously."

"Look, let's not play games." Tears flow down my face once again. "I know you guys were together fucking girls or women.

"This isn't my place to say, Emily. Talk to Josh. I'm single; I can fuck whoever I want."

"Get out!" Sobbing, I lay back on the sofa. "I don't ever want to see you again."

Trevor sat next to me. "You don't have to treat me like that!"

I turn, weeping on his chest. He holds me closely. I sniffle.

"You need to get a grip, Emmy."

"I know; it was just a moment of weakness on my part. It was our honeymoon and he goes to sleep with someone else--not a good way to start a marriage."

"You knew what he was like. I told you he doesn't

love you, Emmy."

"He will, give him time. After he sees our baby he'll be happy, you'll see."

We watch television for a while. Trevor leaves. I go to bed. No Josh. The next day I vomited all morning. Still no Josh. Packing to go home, Josh comes through the door like he didn't sleep all night.

"Where were you?"

"Don't ask me questions, Emily. Just hurry up and pack your stuff. Your dad is waiting for us."

I turn quickly because tears were flowing down my cheeks. Josh is in the shower. I go through his wallet and find girls numbers and notes: *you're a great fuck; could we see each other again.* Josh comes to me. "What the fuck are you doing?" He slaps my face so harshly. I hold my cheeks in shock. That was the first time he hit me, and I doubt it will be the last. "Don't ever be nosy with my personal stuff, you hear?" he yells at me with such anger, and with that we don't say another word.

Emily & Josh

A week passed. Josh hasn't touched me. We're married. It doesn't help living with Mom and Dad, but it doesn't matter; he won't touch me. I'm feeling a much better. Eating has been tough; instead of gaining weight I'm losing weight. All I've been doing is going to school, homework and sobbing–and let's not forget vomiting my guts out.

Mom and Dad are going for date night. They're so in love. I want that kind of love. They look forward to getting all dressed up and going out dinner. Smiling at them, I say, "Goodbye. Have a nice time, Mom, Dad." Having the house to myself was nice until Josh stumbles in drunk. Coming toward me, he grabs my hair.

"Now that your folks aren't here we're going fuck." He is rough and slurring his words. His breath smells of beer. He sticks his tongue down my throat. He's treating me so aggressively it hurts. His breath tastes of cigarettes. Pulling my hair tighter, he drags me to our room and throws me on the bed, staring at me. My heart is thumping for dear life.

"What's wrong with you, Josh?"

"Shut the fuck up!" He starts to rip my blouse. "No bra, slut." Tears flow down my cheeks. Josh doesn't care. He pulls my pants with such force, I felt like I was getting raped.

"Josh, please!"

He slaps my face. I start to shed tears.

"I'm warning, you be quiet, Em." He sucks my breast painfully and lustfully, he sticks two fingers inside my pussy with such force it hurt. "I'm going to bang that pussy hard."

"Remember I'm pregnant, Josh."

I didn't even notice he pulled his pants down, along with his boxers. He forcefully pushes his dick in my sugary spot. I yelled with pain. Banging me roughly, he covers my mouth with his hand. "That's it, Em, shut the fuck up." He moans with his orgasm and leaves me weeping while he takes a shower. Josh grabs my face. "You better not tell anyone about our sex life or I'll beat the shit out of you."

I just nod. "I won't." My words came out with a trembling voice.

"Go be good wife and make some food, lazy bitch."

I go running downstairs to the kitchen and make Josh a meal. I don't know how to cook. I'll do my best. With shaky hands I make pancakes and eggs and a glass of milk. He comes downstairs with no shirt, messy jetblack hair and sweatpants. He frightens me with his yelling. "What the fuck? Pancakes for dinner?" He grabs the plate and throws it against the wall. The food is all over the place. My body starts quivering. "Don't just stand there, you stupid girl; clean up this mess."

I run to fetch a towel.

"I'm going out."

Emily

After I cleaned the mess Josh threw all over the wall and floor my body was sore and shuddering. I went to the bathroom to take a shower. My panty had spots of blood. I scrunched my hand, holding my panty and shedding tears of sadness. Getting in the shower, the water splashing all over my body felt good. I washed my brown long hair, tears flowing with the water spattering my face and body. In bed alone, tears drop on my pillow. I'm not that girl to get hit; what is wrong with me? Depression is creeping in my soul.

I walk to school. My whole body is aching. I didn't even bother putting on makeup but I still lift my head high. Betty is walking my way.

"What's wrong, Emily? You seem under the weather."

"I'm fine--just the baby, that's all. I've been throwing up every day."

"Sorry to hear that, Em. Hope you feel better. Come on let's go eat lunch, okay?"

We eat in the lunch room. Trevor and Josh are talking to girls. Betty just watches me.

"So what's up with you and Rick?"

"We're having sex every day. I'm training him so he could be a sex god."

I start to choke on my milk and it spatters on Betty's face. "Sorry Betts."

"That's ok." We giggle. We're no longer the mean girls we were in school were growing up. Josh never acknowledged me in high school. I'm helping Mom

with dinner, hoping Josh will be here. Wishful thinking--Dad got upset he's never home, I'm in my room doing some homework. At least I'm ahead at school.

Josh comes home. He comes straight to me. "I want to fuck, so take your clothes off and do it now."

"Josh, not tonight."

"Don't make me mad, Em."

"I just don't feel good right now."

"Take off your clothes. I won't ask you again."

With shaking hands I take off my clothes. I'm standing there nude.

"Don't hide your body. I want to see you pleasure yourself."

"I don't want to, Josh!"

Josh gets angry and pushes me on the bed. "Touch your tits."

Biting my bottom lip, I massage my breast. "You can't even be sexy, you pathetic slut."

Tears slowly fall.

"I don't even want you, but my cock needs release." He takes his large penis and just puts it in my sweet spot. I take a deep breath. He doesn't let me have an orgasm; he just turns over and falls asleep. My

aching heart just saddens me with hurt and feeling so
badly.

CHAPTER 5

Emily & Trevor

Months pass. I'm eight months pregnant now. It has been the worst time of my life. Josh didn't help matters either. He was always with his friends and with sluts. He never gave me the time of day. Reality kicked my dreams and hopes out the window, so to speak. I tripled in size with this baby. Josh made fun of me and called me fat slob.

"You're huge, bitch."

Feeling alone, I sobbed every day. I couldn't wait to have this baby. He wouldn't touch me and told me,

"Get out, ugly; you're so unattractive I can't get a boner with that horrible body."

Tears slowly flow down my face and an unpleasant burn went straight to my aching heart. Even my dad and mom hated Josh. They couldn't watch the way he treated me any longer so they rented a one-bedroom duplex.

Trevor came to help move all my stuff. He let his hair grow a bit longer and he had muscles bulging out of his shirt. He always had a nice body. He always works out. I'm so embarrassed. He just stares at me and my belly. It is so huge. I go pick up a box.

"Hey Em, you can't pick up that box."

"Want to make a bet?"

"Let me help you!"

"Thanks Trevor."

"You really look beautiful."

"You don't have to say that!"

"It's true."

"Look at me--I'm huge."

"You're having a baby, Em; it's natural to gain weight."

"Josh says…"

"Who cares what he says? Em, to me you're beautiful."

"Thanks for saying that, Trevor."

"It's ok, baby girl, don't cry for him. He's not worth your tears."

I sob on Trevor's chest and he holds me with all of his strength. I haven't been caressed in such a long time. It felt good, familiar and yet he's the wrong guy. My heart was for Josh; just maybe I could change him someday. There is always tomorrow--that's what Scarlet told herself in *Gone with the Wind*. Rhett also her he didn't give a damn. I loved that classic movie.

Josh didn't come home. Trevor held me throughout the movie. He bought pizza. All of a sudden I was having contractions. "Oh my God!"

"What's wrong, Emily?"

"I'm going to have my baby. Please take me to the

hospital."

"Okay, baby girl."

"Hurry!" Tears are gushing down my face. The pain was pure torment and discomfort. Trevor stayed with me the entire time I had my baby boy. He was incredibly beautiful, with dark brown hair and brown eyes. He didn't look like his dad; he looked more like me.

"He's cute, Em."

"Thank you so much, Trevor; you are a life saver."

He just gives me a sad smile.

"You want to hold him?"

"All right." He holds my son with a firm grip when it was Josh that was supposed be here. All I could do is smile at them, my heart full of excitement for my baby. Trevor leaves when Mom and Dad walk in. Of course, Dad asks for Josh. Finally Dad holds Travis Maxwell and forgets about Josh.

Trevor & Josh

Trevor finds Josh in bed with some slut when Emily giving's birth to his baby.

"Hey jackass, Emily gave birth to your son."

"Who cares?"

I grab the girl and throw her out.

"What the fuck, dude?"

"Get your clothes and go see your wife and child."

"Don't tell me what to do, stupid fuck!"

"I honestly knew you were an asshole to stoop this low--downright mean. Your son is beautiful."

"Then you should've stayed with her."

"I did because you were too busy with a slut that doesn't give a shit about you."

"So what? Why are you all over my shit?"

"Emily and your son are not shit."

"Get the fuck out of my life, asshole."

BROKEN DREAMS

"Her mom and dad were there--just a heads-up."

All I could do is think about Emily. How could Josh be so cold? This isn't my business anyway. I've just got to detach myself from them.

Josh fell asleep for a while. I just showered and ate some chips with salsa and drank a beer or maybe three, then went to some friend's house to smoke some pot. Josh didn't want to go see Emily and the baby. All he cared about was fucking random chicks. And here they come, five chicks, all different shapes and sizes.

Trevor seemed like he was thinking about few things, probably about Em. We didn't care; we were getting wasted playing cards. Alex tells us let's play strip poker. We got the girls' attention. We're all at the table. Trevor is shuffling the cards. We're ready and there is so much tension; all us guys wanting lust and to be fucked, one by one. Trevor was laughing. I didn't have a shirt and my shoes. Josh had all his clothes. Alex just had his boxers on. The chicks only had their bras and panties. I was licking my lips with anticipation and my eager cock was growing under the table like a jackin-the-box toy when you turn it over and over again and the clown pops out--that's how my cock will pop.

One of the chicks was nude and turned on the music. She started to slow dance and all of us guys couldn't focus on the game. She had a nice body, with full C-cup breasts--well they looked like a C cup; what do I know--small waist, blonde hair in a bun. She slowly let it down and started touching herself, swaying with the rhythm of the soft music. Josh gets up grabs, her takes and her to one of the rooms.

All the guys start laughing; with a hard on it was even funnier. The chicks were giggling like girls. My cock is growing by the minute; her tits are bouncing up and down. I couldn't take it any longer. I get the cute red head. Her body was very curvy and she was nude; that's all I needed.

"Alex, I'm going to use your room, okay dude?"

"Have fun," he grins.

I hold the red head's hand like a guy should. She liked that. You get more out of girls when you treat them with a little dignity--you know, a sense of pride. Truth be told, I learned the hard way about chicks. She gets on the bed and spreads wide.

"Sorry, get on your knees and suck my massive cock."

She kind of pouted but when I take my dick, she opens her eyes wide because the head is a mouthful.

"Suck that bad boy."

She does what I say. I lay on the bed with the red head on top, sucking her melons, all so sweet. Her sounds of pleasure were making me senseless. She was in control of this ride. We both had our pleasure and we had shameless laughter and fucked again.

Emily

I stayed in the hospital for a day and half with my baby boy in my arms, crying non-stop.

Not knowing what to do or how to be a mom, I started to sob myself. Josh didn't come home to see his son. Just maybe he'll come today and that's a huge maybe. Baby Travis fell asleep and I was so exhausted fell asleep for a couple of hours when *bang*! The door opens and Josh comes in. Travis starts to cry loud enough to wake the dead; they say if they cry their lung develop better. Then Josh gets angry. "Shut that baby up."

"Why don't you go see your son, Josh?"

"He's your son, not mine."

"You are so mean, Josh."

"I'm too young for this, Em."

"Well, I am too! You are a father now."

"Get out of my way; got to go to class. We do go to school, you know, and I'm going to look for a job so get used to me not being here."

He showers and leaves me alone with the baby once again. He didn't even look at him or carry our baby. All I could do was cry and be depressed. Betty comes to my little duplex with a gift. She's beautiful, with her long silky blonde hair, swaying her beautiful body. My stomach is huge from the baby.

"Travis is so cute. He looks like you, not Josh. Where is he?"

"Where else? With his friends. He said he was looking for a job, but he knows he could work for his dad."

"You'll be all right, Em."

"Thanks Betts."

"I have to go; Rick is waiting."

"How is that working out? Tell me; I'm so bored."

"Ok, don't tell anyone, but Rick and I had sex and he was a virgin--really. If he knew how many guys I fucked…"

"So tell me you love Rick; it wasn't just a fuck."

"He was so cute. He has a huge dick, so satisfying. I showed him what makes me tick."

"I bet you did." We start giggling.

"He's really a fast learner. I sucked his cock. He loved it so much he came all over my mouth, dripping all over my neck."

"Wow! That good, huh?" My eyes rolled back in my head. *She always gets what and who she wants. It's not fair,* I say to myself.

Two months passed. I got my figure back. Travis was so adorable. He was a good boy and didn't cry so much anymore. Josh was going to school and working, so I didn't see him much. Mom took care of Travis when I went to school so I could graduate. I miss my baby boy.

I was eating when Trevor came to sit with me.

"Hey, beautiful."

"Hi Trevor."

"You're looking good. Your breasts got larger and your body is different."

I roll my eyes. "Is that all you have to say?"

"Just giving you a compliment." His face gets red.

"Sorry, just a bit moody."

"What you need is a good fuck."

"Thanks, I needed to hear that." All I could do was look down at my food that I wasn't eating.

Trevor

I couldn't take my eyes off Emily. It's always heartwrenching to watch the way Josh treats her like shit. I want her. There is something about her that rocks my boat. We're graduating in a few weeks. She's more beautiful than ever. I will go to Alex's party after. Who knows if she'll get to go? She's been going to school and taking care of the baby. I go to help but it just seems I make matters worse. I can feel the intensity when I'm near her. I'm fucking lots of girls so I can forget Em but the damn girl is in my veins and my soul. She must never find out that I want her badly. She's like a drug and I need my fix one way or another.

Meanwhile I'm horny as hell. I'm going to Alex's house; he always has girls there. Alex is sitting on the sofa while a chick is sucking his junk. I go to the fridge to get a beer and stand next to the sink until he blows his load inside that cute chick's mouth. Some pretty girl comes to the kitchen and smiles.

"Hi, I'm Candy."

"Trevor. Nice to meet you, Candy. They're getting busy on the sofa; it's like watching a porn movie. Have a beer, Cindy."

"It's Candy."

"Sorry, my bad. Want to go upstairs with me, Candy? I'll show you my huge beef pole."

She grins. "Sure, why not? I got hot and bothered hearing them."

BROKEN DREAMS

We go to Alex's bedroom. This chick is cute, with black wavy hair and huge jugs. She's kind of chucky but who cares? She wakes me out of my thoughts.

"Let's see that huge beef pole."

"Sure thing, sweetie; come over here and let me show you." I take her blouse off and snap her bra off. Those jugs hit my cheek. Fuck, while I'm sucking her tits she makes this high-pitched sound. It was annoying. I wanted her to shut up and let me fuck her so I laid her down on the bed and removed her pants with her panties. I didn't want to touch her breasts because she'll make those funny sounds. All I wanted was my release. What I really wanted was to put a pillow over her face and smother her to shut her up. I'm a guy that shouldn't be complaining how girls make noises. There's just one girl whose sounds are amazing, and that would be Emily.

CHAPTER 6

Emily & Trevor

Mom, could I go to a party after graduation? Everyone is going. Could you take care of Travis?"

"I don't mind taking care of Travis. I just worry about you Em. Josh is never with you."

"He works, Mom, and he's been going to school."

"Okay sweetie, you can go. You haven't gone out for a while. You go have fun after you graduate. Dad and I will take you to dinner."

"Thanks Mom, I love you so much." We hug. My

mom is wonderful.

Josh didn't go to the dinner with my parents, of course. My dad was furious; in reality he should be used to it. My dad and mom gave me money as a gift. It's so awesome; they're paying for my rent. Bless them for helping me. They truly love me. I am the only child.

I go with Betty and Rick to the party feeling like the third wheel. Josh wasn't around but he will be at the party for sure. The party is in full swing, with guys and girls drinking, I want to get really drunk. Why not? My life is so pathetic; being a mother changes everything. Just one night I want to be a young girl having fun.

Scoping the scene, I see her. She looks beautiful: long brown hair flowing in curls, wearing a fitted black sweater with a short black skirt that shouldn't be legal, black stocking upper thighs–fuck, my cock is stirring in my pants; wanting her was an understatement. Emily is drinking. Where is Josh, that asshole, leaving her with Betty and Rick? I lean against the wall just staring at her so that no one will touch her, drinking my beer. Some girl that I fucked last week--fuck my life, she's in my way and I can't watch Em.

"Trevor, want to dance?"

"No thanks, I just want to be alone."

"You didn't want to be alone last week. I roll my eyes. She leaves pissed and all I can do is watch Emily, why I just don't know! A guy is approaching her, that fucker, and she has the nerve to smile to him. That's it; I'm taking her out of here. I grab her arm.

"Hey! What are you doing, Trevor?"

"Taking you home."

"I'm here with Betts and Rick."

"I don't care."

"Stop it, you're hurting my arm."

"Well, stop moving around."

"I don't want to go home, Trevor."

"Well, I can't take you to my house; my mom is home."

I take her to an awful old motel. I hated to do it, but I want her so badly. As soon we were in the room I bang her in the wall.

She gasps, "What are you doing?"

"Sorry you, beautiful diamond, you're going to be mine tonight."

I start devouring her delicious lips. I swallow her breath; I couldn't help it. I couldn't stop myself. She moans; she probably can't breathe. I pull her sweater above her head. Her hair flows down. She has on a white lace bra. I lift her skirt up; my hands smooth her body. She whimpers; she's driving me insane.

Trevor & Emily

I still have Em against the wall and my snake is growing by the minute. She starts to say something like 'I can't do this!' Once again I kiss her roughly; she's not going to tell me no!

"You want this, Em; you want to be devoured as much as I want to stick my dick in your tight tunnel."

I carry her to the bed. Her skirt goes up, revealing her white lace bikini panties. I pull them off quickly. With her tan skin, she's so beautiful. My tongue goes to her sweet spot; her hands go straight to my hair. She pulls; her moans are incredible. She wants me. I voraciously eat her pussy; it almost consumes me.

"Oh Trevor, it feels good, please!! Oh! Please! I'm coming," she yells.

"I'm not finished with you, sweet diamond." I suck on her breasts; her nipples are pink. Getting on top of her, my huge snake knows where to go in her tight pussy. Grabbing her hips toward me, I pump hard.

"Oh! Yeah! Baby, that's it, harder, come with me, precious diamond; come on, harder."

We came with such power, we were sweating. It felt wonderful. We slept in each other's arms. The reality hits me: she's not mine to keep. She's his. That makes me sad because I have to give her back. Hating the way I'm feeling, it's bittersweet kissing her mouth while she's still sleeping. All I do is watch her sleep. I wanted to tell her my emotions for so long but she won't leave Josh and she truly loves him. She's only with me because he doesn't love her; he never did. Josh will always love Abby and because he let her go, he will make Emily miserable, hurt and break her down. That makes me want to hate him but he's my best friend. Holding her tighter I fall in a deep sleep.

I feel like I'm suffocating, needing some air to breathe because Trevor is holding me with all his might. I need to leave, but his hold on me feels nice. It's been a while someone held me like that! We may be young but that doesn't mean we don't have feelings. Trevor is still sleeping. Putting my clothes, I leave. I have a baby boy to worry about and my mom might be concerned, so I leave and call Betty to pick me up. Of course, Rick got upset. They took me home.

Rick & Betty

"Why did Emily leave the party, Betts? Then hours later she wants us to pick her up. Who knows what and whom she was with."

"Don't be concerned about Em; be more concerned about your girlfriend that has needs. I'm so horny for you, baby. My muffin is so wet for you, baby."

"Betts, you're always hot to trot."

"Remember how I showed you to tie me and suck my muffin? Do it now."

"You're relentless, Betts."

"I can't help it, Ricky. I love your large rod, baby."

Taking off my jeans and shirt, I pull her hair like she wants me to. "I'm banging you hard, baby. Where's the rope?"

"Over in my dresser."

I tie her wrists. She's nude. My eyes light up like

fire; my body is burning for her. She's such a guy's dreams come true; she does whatever you want. She teaches me everything so I could satisfy her every need. Sucking her bare pussy was like tasting a slurping vanilla ice cream, but better. Licking her clean was making my huge rod expand even more. As she screams out loud, I untie her and lie on the bed. Betts is sucking my cock in no time; she's a great cocksucker. She likes me to cum all over her mouth sometimes. I wonder if she loves sex more than guys do? She moans and I roar; my cum is dripping out of her mouth. She rubs some on her tits and face because girls from school told her it's a great facial cream. I laughed when she told me. We take a shower and sleep in each other's arms.

I always wondered what happened to Abby. Is she all right; did something happen to her? Is she happy? Does she think of me at least once? One day out of the blue, she just vanishes. I miss her. Life goes on, whether we like it or not. Betty stirs, waking up.

"Why are you awake, Ricky? Are you thinking of her again?"

"Don't start with that, Betts! Just because I can't sleep doesn't mean I'm thinking of Abby."

"Okay, could we have some more sex then?"

"You really are relentless, girl. Get over here."

We have an intense encounter of lust in our young age. Betts is every guy's dream but sometimes she goes beyond any guy's expectation. I'm really starting to like her as a sex partner and friend, for now anyway. Maybe something could come from this friendship. We're still young to think of all of those emotions. All I want to do is explore my wild oats because to tell you the truth, Betty has a sex addiction. I just hope I can keep up with her and that hot, tight pussy.

Emily & Josh

I came home late that night after that encounter with Trevor McQueen. Josh was waiting for me. His face showed he was very angry.

"Where the fuck have you been, Emmy? Who gave you permission to go out?"

"Josh, don't start, please!"

"You know, bitch, you're asking to get your ass spanked. Where is the baby? Where else--with your mother. Where were you and who were you with, Emmy?"

"I went to a party with Rick and Betty."

Unexpectedly he slaps my face. Tears slowly fall down my face.

Then he grabs my hair and pulls me to him. "Don't ever go anywhere without my consent, do you understand?"

All I could do is nod. He was pulling my hair tight toward him. "Please don't, Josh. I'm really tired."

"I bet you're tired. I have needs, bitch. Since you're my wife and all, go take a shower and wait for me in our bed."

I go quickly; I don't want to get him any angrier than he is. Taking a shower felt so good, water spraying my sore body after having sex with Trevor. I wrap my towel around my body. Josh is waiting for me. His bulge is huge.

"I bought you a black short skirt. Every time we have sex, you wear it!"

With trembling hands I put on the skimpy skirt without a bra. "Ok." My voice was weak. I hate being at his mercy. To my surprise he wraps me around him, giving kisses all over my body. He made me come to life. I wanted him to fuck me, to take me out of my thoughts as he pleases me. Yeah, I'm pathetic and I know we have a dysfunctional relationship. At this point I didn't care; he wakes my thoughts with sexual arousal. He licks my vagina with that hungry tongue and my desire increases. My blood flows. His penis is hard and I want it so badly. Yes, it feels so good. My heart is beating faster and faster. I'm ready to come and my orgasm subsides.

"Get on top Emmy."

I do what he says; he's pinching my nipples and I ride him. He gets rough. We both come with no clemency, just two broken people with no rules or hope.

CHAPTER 7

Emily

Three months later I'm pregnant again. What am I going to do and who is the father? I slept with both of them; is it Trevor or Josh? Josh hasn't touched me since that night and my baby Travis is six months. Now I have to tell Josh. I tell my mom; all she can do is make a sad face of disappointment.

"Sorry Mom, I was taking care of myself. It was just meant to be. I didn't do it on purpose."

Josh and I are having dinner. He always leaves when he finishes.

"I need to talk, Josh."

"About what, Emmy?"

"There is something I need to say."

"Well, say it already." He drops his fork on the plate. "Well, I'm waiting."

Biting my lip has been my nervous reaction these days. "I'm pregnant."

"What the fuck?" He bangs the table with his fist. "What are you, a baby machine now?"

"I'm sorry. I was on the pill."

"Fuck, what are we going to do, Emily?"

"What do you mean? I'm going to have our baby, Josh."

"Well then, you're on your own."

"Why do you have to be cruel all the time?"

"I'm going out; don't wait up either."

My tears slide effortlessly down my cheeks. He is so awful to me. I feel lost in my so-called life. Reality kicks in when Travis cries. "What's wrong, baby boy?"

He's nine months old now. He's getting big and so

cute. It's going to be tough going to night school. My mom has been an angel helping me, but I won't stop going to school.

Two weeks have passed. I'm getting morning sickness and Josh is giving me the cold shoulder. Betty, my best friend, came to hug me a few times. Sobbing is all I can do these days, and to put the icing on the cake, Travis got sick and was up all night crying. He was vomiting and I, along with him. Life is tough right now but I'm strong. I think it's for the best because this is insane. My broken dreams are shattering before my eyes. There's a knock. I tiptoe toward the door. Travis finally fell asleep. When I opened the door Trevor is all sexy, standing there with a grin that makes my knees wobble. All I could think is how handsome he is; just the thought of him caressing me gives me tingles through my body.

Trevor & Emily

"What are you doing here?"

"Josh told me you're pregnant again."

"Well, if he told you, why come to tell me about your conversation?"

"We slept together; is that baby mine?"

"No, it's not. I fucked Josh as soon as I came; he is my husband, you know."

"And what am I, Em, your fuck buddy?" I wanted to hug her, throw her in the bed and make sweet love but she isn't mine to love or devour. If she knew what Josh was doing it would make her so heartbroken. I'm sure she knows there's a different girl; she doesn't have to see the actual act to knowing that he is cheating on her every chance he gets. We even did a threesome the other day.

"Do you want a soda?"

"Sure, I could use some company."

We take a seat on the sofa. "How is Community College?"

"It's good. How is night school, Em?"

"Fine. I miss Travis but Mom has been great."

"If you ever need help babysitting I'm more than happy to oblige."

"Are you sure with that busy schedule of school and fucking random chicks?"

"I am single, you know."

"Yeah, I know." Emily is pouting, her brown eyes filled with sorrow. I can't do anything to stop it.

"Come here, Em; let me hold you. We are friends."

She comes to me like this is what she was yearning for, and I hold her tight with all my might. I want to tell her, "Love me not him; he will destroy you," but I keep it inside because she is not my treasure. As I am lost in my thoughts, she falls asleep. I make her dinner and take care of Travis. He is truly adorable. He is cuddly, probably yearning for male attention, poor guy. I feel we're connecting in some way.

"Wow! Trevor, thanks for taking care of my baby boy."

"You needed a break, Em, I guess."

We eat together. She's wearing shorts and a loose t-shirt. I can't stop staring at her. She's so naturally tan, with silky brown hair I wanted to put my fingers through. Pregnant or not, I want her so badly it hurts not to touch her body, to only see her once in a while. My heart is in pain yet wanting other girls or women is not fair for her. She has an asshole already; she doesn't need another but my heart wants her. I will savor whatever she can give me. I'll be that guy she runs to or sleeps with--anything for Emily. I'll be the fall guy.

"I have to leave, E." I kiss her forehead.

She holds my arm and whispers, "Don't go."

"What do you want, babe?"

"I haven't had sex since that night we had sex, and later with Josh. After that day he didn't touch me. The baby is asleep."

"What about Josh? He might come home."

"He won't."

I could never deny her; God only knows I won't try, either. I take her t-shirt off. Her breasts are already plump there's something to be said about a pregnant woman or in her case young girl. We get it on and what wonderful fulfillment it was--amazing.

Josh & Emily

We are driving around because Josh got lost and of course, he's angry with me, like it's my fault. His dad asked him to pick up some parts, since his dad owns a forklift company. Josh works with him so he can pay our rent while I go to night school. Josh really hates working with his dad but he has to.

"Josh, we're going around circles."

He slaps my face. I truly didn't see that coming. My nose starts to bleed. Travis starts to cry. My tears stream down my face--what else is new? I'm a crybaby these days; my hormones are going wild.

"You see what you made me do, bitch? Shut that that kid up."

I stay silent. I don't want to make him more furious. Feeling my face swollen and in pain, feeling stuck in this situation, I can change him one day, I know! I can; we're still young. We never found the place. He left me at home with a swollen nose. Someone is knocking. I'm hoping it's not Mom or Dad; if they see me like this...

Well, only one way to find out. It's Betts.

"Hi girlfriend--hey, what happened to you?"

"Clumsy me--I hit my nose on the door."

"God, Emmy, be careful. You have time to talk?"

"Sure, what's up?"

"How are you, Em? You look lifeless."

"Thanks, just what I needed to hear."

"Sorry, I just worry about you."

"Boy, you have time to worry about me? I'm impressed, Betts."

"Don't be sarcastic."

"Sorry, what brings you here?"

"Ok, I'm going to tell you the truth."

"That would be nice."

"Trevor asked me to come."

"For what?"

"He was worried about you."

"Well, tell him not to be!"

"Does he have something to worry about, Emmy?"

"No, he doesn't." I won't let anyone know that Josh beats me. I don't want anyone's pity. I'm strong.

"Emmy, I'm talking to you!"

"What?"

"Are you really ok? You seem far way."

"Let's not talk about me. How are you doing with Rick?"

"Between you and me, all he thinks about is her."

"About whom?"

"About Abby, who else? I can't stand it; she's not around anymore! Rick loves her, not me; he will never love me. I still have fun fucking him and all the guys that are willing to feed my appetite."

I just wanting to roll my eyes but I don't; this is her life.

I was feeding Travis when Josh comes in. "Get in the room, Emmy."

"I'm feeding Travis."

"Put him in the bed. Do it now."

"No!"

"What? You're fucking talking back to me?" He grabs Travis and puts him in his bed and the baby starts crying. He pulls my hair, drags me into our bedroom and throws me on the bed. Tears are flowing down my cheeks. He ripped my panty; more tears flood my cheeks. He slaps my sore face. I am sobbing so badly. He pulls my hair.

"What's wrong with you? Go put that black   skirt on now! Do it."

With shaking hands and trembling body, I put on that rag of a skirt that turns him on.

"You're already getting fat."

"I'm pregnant, Josh."

"Shut the fuck up and get on the end of the bed." He fucks me hard. My face aches; my body is numb. All I do is close my eyes and wait for him to finish.

Emily

Months pass so quickly. I didn't gain that much weight with all the abuse. No one knew what was going on. It would be so embarrassing if anyone found out. I'm not that girl. I used to be the mean girl, remember, until Abby kicked my ass. She was a feisty bitch. Well, I shouldn't have been talking like a bully. We treated her awful. It wasn't her fault that Rick and Josh loved her, but she was so plain Jane. Who knows why? We'll never know; I'm guessing what you can't have, you want. I'm nine months. Josh went to Vegas. I begged him not to go; I wasn't feeling good. His jaw clenched and my stomach did a somersault--not in a good way, either. He just gives me a warning not to speak. Everyone went. Betty, of course, was the main dish; even Trevor went, and Rick. They're all having fun. I'm stuck at home. Tears pour down my face. Feeling sorry for myself is the norm these days. I go to the fridge for some ice cream.

I'm going to watch *From Here to Eternity*. It's a 1953 classic that just fits my mood. Lying on the sofa eating my vanilla ice cream, I was in the middle of the movie when I got my first pain. Oh my God! I'm going to call my mom. I'm going for the phone when a sharp pain rips my body in agony. There's a knock. Maybe it's Mom. I walk slowly.

"Trevor, what are you doing here? I thought you

went to Vegas with Josh. Oh my God!" Another pain hits. "Emily, what's wrong?"

"I'm having the baby, please help me." I'm holding my stomach. "Call my mom to come for Travis, ok?"

I'm in the hospital with so much pain I just wanted to die. Trevor is holding my hand with a sad smile.

"I wish could take this pain away from you, Em." My tears gush; he wipes them away and kisses my lips. "Everything's going to be ok babe."

Another kiss from his wonderful lips, and the pain comes back. There's no time to reminisce. They rush me to a sanitized room, then my miracle happens. My baby girl cries. Trevor even had tears.

"She's beautiful Em."

She looks like Travis: chocolate brown eyes, honey brown hair, light skin--must have gotten that from her dad. Travis has tan skin; that's the only difference between them. Brother and sister look alike.

Josh was a no-show. I called his hotel and a girl answered. I just hung up. Why bother? I mean, Em will always count on me. Watching her with the baby was the most beautiful sight I've ever seen. Staring at Emily feeding her baby girl, I ask, "What are you going to name her?"

"I'm going to call her Trina Owen."

"That's a nice name, Em."

"Thanks."

Her distressed face breaks my heart.

CHAPTER 8

Emily

Years passed like the wind and five kids later, Josh called me a baby machine. I had to tell the doctor to do something. He told me tubal ligation was over 99% effective. I didn't waste any time. I told mom to take the kids for two days. Josh didn't want anything to do with me at this point. That hurt very much. I was determined to change him. When I had our third baby Josh was so in love with him. I named him Wade Maxwell. He had the feature of Kyle, his brother, and Wade was the lucky kid; he's the only one that got love in that household. I gave my children lots of love but with the abuse and Josh's frequent beatings…the last beating broke my arm and my nose. I lie to everyone. That is my pathetic life. I finished community college in business but I couldn't work. Having five children made it hard. All the kids were going to school now; they were older, which made it a bit easier. I heard that Trevor McQueen was sleeping with every woman he could find, along with Josh; they're best friends after all. Betty was going to some bar called Cocky Bull. They had karaoke. I never could go because having four boys and one girl was tough.

The last two boys, Jett Maxwell and Jack Maxwell, looked so much like Josh: jet-black hair, light-skinned, with gray-blue eyes. Wade had green eyes like Josh's brother Kyle, with jet-black hair and tan skin. All my children are beautiful. Sometimes I wonder if the life I was giving them was right. They've seen Josh hit me so many times and they would cry. The sadness in their small faces now there older is awful.

Betty called me. She married Rick, the love of her life, so why does she keep going out with Josh and Trevor? Rick has his own company. He told me so many times he would like me to work there. I know he was being nice. I went sobbing with the kids and once or twice we stayed the weekend. I'm very tired of my life. My life has been anything but happiness, I'm so depressed when I see myself in the mirror; all I see is a woman with broken dreams and a shattered heart. Mom came for the kids so I could go out for a while. Wearing a tight black dress, very short, I'm getting laid tonight. I don't know how long I haven't been with a real man.

Betty & Emily

Walking in Cocky Bull--well, it's very old, with broken Christmas lights, women trying to get free drinks, men thinking they're getting laid and lots of cute guys and men. Betty and I went to have a seat. All eyes are on Betts. I guess I'm not pretty enough. Suddenly I didn't want to be here. I tell my friend I can't stay.

"Em, we just got here."

"See you later." I run out of the bar, gasping for air. Someone grabs my arm roughly and throws me into the car. He hits me in the face; I fall back on the seat. I was dizzy. He was saying to shut up or he'll kill me. Tears run down my face. He parks in an alley. "All I want is to fuck you so give me what I want and you live; it's that simple."

"Please don't, please!"

He slaps my face once again; he takes a blade and takes my clothes off. The car is huge, maybe a limousine or something. He starts to touch my breast with the blade. My sobs get worse by the minute. He strikes my face he bites my nipples, and I yell. He presses my mouth and licks my whole face--so disgusting. All I wanted was to for him to get off me.

He takes his cock out and makes me suck him. I started to choke. He kept pulling my hair. Finally, he rapes me in the roughest way. All I could see is his green eyes because he had a mask. After he finishes he throws me out of the car to the ground. I hit cement with a thump. He leaves me there nude. He at least threw my clothes out. I didn't move, crying. I must have passed out. I woke up in a hospital bed with tears on my pillow on my side because I didn't want to see anyone. My body ached. I felt dirty.

I heard Trevor say, "Where is she?"

"You're not family."

"So what? She's my friend!" Trevor barged in. "Baby girl." He runs to me. I let go of all my sorrow on his chest; he holds me until I have no more tears; all I have is emptiness. He kisses my forehead. "When I found out you went to Cocky Bull, I went to take care of you. When I got there you were gone."

"He raped me, Trevor; I won't be the same anymore."

"Don't say that, Em; you're strong, baby girl."

"Get out! I hate you!"

"You don't mean that!"

"Yes I do, leave me alone."

"What's going on here?"

"Mom!"

She runs to me and hugs me like a mom who loves her baby girl. Mom eventually asks Trevor to leave. With his sad face he rushes out. I was grateful, sobbing; the rapist took something that night. Everyone takes from me; I get nothing in return, ever. All I get is beaten, raped, mistreated--maybe I'm getting punished for being a mean girl in school. That was the past. I'm not a little girl anymore, just a woman and a mother with a broken heart and broken dreams.

Trevor & Rick

I go to Rick's house. They walk to the park.

"What's up, dude?"

"Emily got raped last night."

"What?"

"Betty took her to Cocky Bull. Emily is not like Betty."

"Are you blaming Betts? This isn't her fault."

"Why would she take her there? We all know people go there to get fucked and wildly drunk. Those asshole are always sticking their dicks…"

"Look, I know you're upset and that you really care about Emily, but could you eases up on Betty? She said once she went inside the bar she panicked and she ran out, not waiting for Betts to go after her."

"I need to go drink; want to go?"

"Sure! Why not?"

BROKEN DREAMS

We walk in Cocky Bull. Taking a seat we ask for two shots and some beers. The jukebox is playing *Looking for love in all the wrong places* by Johnny Lee. Trevor smirks and Rick laughs remembering Betts and Em went wild over that movie.

I continue to drink. "Why Rick? She's so broken."

"It's okay, Trevor; she's tough."

"You didn't see her; she told me she hated me!"

"Come on man, she hates any man. She was raped. She'll be all right. She has five kids that will help her; if there's one thing about Em, she loves her kids."

"What about Josh? He treats her so wrong."

"He's a jackass but that's his wife, Trevor."

"She needs love, and someone to take good care of her."

"You're not that man. Stay away from her, Trevor."

I drink some more. A girl comes next to me.

"Hi, could you buy me a drink?" She kind of looks like Emily.

"Sure, what would you like?"

"A margarita."

"You heard the lady, Ben." He nods. Rick calls Betty; she tells Rick to meet her at the house. She's been with Emily.

Trevor is getting drunk for sure. He's going to fuck this woman; she's all over him. She's sitting on his lap, rubbing her ass back and forth. They'll be in the restroom in no time. As soon as I thought it, he tells me he's going to the back. The cute woman follows him. I don't want him to go home drunk by himself, so I stay, drinking a beer and talking to Ben. I don't look around because the women are horny. I'm a faithful man and I want to stay that way.

"Wow! Trevor, you have a huge cock."

"You like it? Well, suck it then." We're in the back. There's a room we all rent to save on hotels. That's good for the guys and for the girls we fuck. I'm against the wall. She zips down my zipper oh so slowly. Man, she's licking her lips. "Mercy."

"That's not my name, Trevor." She made me roll my eyes just sucking. She starts to lick. Man, she's biting the head of my cock. Moaning, I pull her hair. She's sucking my cock like she's starving. Yeah! I stop her. I put a condom on. Putting her against the wall, pulling her blouse sucking her tits, licking, biting– yeah!

"Baby, suck my melons hard. Yeah! Please, harder." I stick my huge shaft in her tight pussy and I bang her all the way in. Her legs around my waist, me holding her waist--we come with such intense climax.

Emily

Months pass, and the storm is still here with me and my empty existence since I got raped. My kids needed me or I would've wanted to die. The days felt slow. I didn't talk to anyone or see anyone. I lost myself that night my broken dreams were shattered before my eyes. Josh hasn't helped; he's never home. I felt it was a blessing Josh not being home. I hate everyone just about now! I'm sobbing every day and all night. I have no human contact, just my five kids. They're older now. Travis is a doll, helping me and taking care of me. I was so grateful.

"Mom, could you join us to watch a movie?" Travis wakes me from my thoughts. I say yes because I can't say no to my son. He's already fifteen years old. The other kids follow; I had them so close. Wade has given me so many problems because Josh just spoiled him. He's only eleven. Trina is thirteen and the other two are Jake and Jason. We all go to the sofa as a family and we watch *Family Vacation*. We laugh and make popcorn. When the door bangs, we all jump. Josh calls me to the room. Like a dummy I go, not thinking of anything. To tell you the truth, I don't care what he does to me. I still remember when we went to Betty and Rick's wedding. It was on top of a hill at some beautiful restaurant. Mom took care of the kids for me. Josh was drinking so much we started to fight and he pushed me down the hill. My new dress was ruined, along with my pride and dignity. I never knew why he was angry. I started to hate my life with a passion. I have to admit I would've taken my life if it wasn't for my kids. My life was pitiful. I never knew what was going to happen next. This wasn't the life I dreamed of; all I have is broken dreams with the one man I ever loved, who is the man that beat me, humiliated me, and made me feel unimportant. Who does this much hurt to someone who loves him? Love is not supposed to hurt, yet my heart is in so many pieces. What can I do? No one will ever want to love me with so many kids. I'm a damaged woman with no self-worth.

"I'm talking to you, bitch."

"Stop Josh, the kids are listening."

"I'm saying you better go back to work. We need money."

"So you could fuck those girls or do whatever you

do with them."

He grabs my hair. "Shut the fuck up!"

I gasp, "Please Josh."

He runs to the door and locks it. "You're not going to get away with talking to me like that!" Josh starts beating me. "You stupid whore." He punches my face, slaps, kicks and hits me until I bleed. He leaves me in the floor and takes the little bit of money I had left.

Darkness hits me.

CHAPTER 9

Trevor & Josh

Trevor asks Josh, "What took you so long? Why do you look like you got in a fight?"

"I don't want to talk about it. Betty is waiting for us."

Josh looks up at Trevor. "Are you sure you want to fuck your best friend's wife?"

"You want to back off? She has a huge hunger for sex and Rick is not enough for her. She's waiting in a nice hotel; let's go! I can't wait to hit that tight pussy. I was told she liked threesomes. This is not her first rodeo, if you know what I mean. Let's get some drugs."

We both smirk. When we knock at the hotel Betty opens the door wearing a short leather skirt and a silk blouse.

"Well, are you coming in or just going to gawk at me?"

We go in. It's a pretty fancy place. We don't care; we like fucking dirty woman in dirty hotels. Betts puts on music and some hard core porn. She has it on silent. She makes drinks for us.

"You don't care that you're going to fuck your best friend's husband?"

"Let's keep this under wraps. No one has to get hurt. Come on boys; we'll drink then we can fuck our brains out! That's if you can take me." We both grin.

"Ready boys? Come get me."

We go to the room--very nice silk sheets and strawberries on the small table, with drinks, whipped cream and rope--fuck yeah! We're ready. Josh and I look at each other.

"Trevor gets the front; you, baby, get my backside."

"I wouldn't have it any other way, sweetie," Josh says.

She turns on the porn again, like we needed it. She licks her lips. We help her take her blouse. She has on a sheer bra with all these sparkles. Trevor starts to suck her tits; they're beautiful. Josh takes his time removing her short leather skirt. Fuck, she has a firm ass with a sheer g-string.

"I'm going to tear that ass up."

She giggles. "You guys are amateurs."

"You won't be saying that later; you'll want our cocks every single day."

Trevor lies on his back. Betty puts her pussy in his face. She's holding the bed frame while Josh licks her ass. It reeks of sex. Tasting her juices is fantastic. She was holding her release; she was a pro at this.

Josh speaks up. "Let me lick that pussy."

They take turns, Trevor squeezing her tits and

pinching her nipples while Josh licks her clean. She comes fiercely and whimpers with satisfaction, her lips parted. She starts to suck both our cocks. We're both standing in front of her, of course, one at a time. She licks with hunger. Betty's groans are impossible to ignore. We come all over her. What a sight to see! I was getting hard again while she licked our huge cocks, standing in front of us, cum dripping from her mouth and down her chin. It was amazing; I can't wait to fuck her once more. The night was still young. We tie her up to the bedpost. Now it was Trevor's turn to tap that firm ass, while Josh was on his back. Each of her arms was stretched out while Josh was sucking her breasts and Trevor was fucking her backside.

Trevor & Josh

The sex escapade was still going strong. Now we got down and dirty. She was licked, finger fucked and tongue fucked. We tied her up. She really loves hard core sex. We kissed her lips while Josh put some kind of lubricant on his cock. We were ready. Trevor was lying down. She was facing him once again while he licked and sucked her nipples, sliding his huge rod in her tight pussy. Once he was inside her warm twat, Josh slid his rod in her ass. She was in full swing with our huge dicks "Yeah! That's good, boys, very good."

We chuckle because we're not boys anymore. We move slowly, she moans, "Harder, please."

We start to bang her in and out; she took us like a beautiful slut.

Josh went home; I stayed with Betty. That's how we started our affair. We sneaked without Rick knowing we fuck everywhere. I didn't see Emily or ask about her. She wasn't mine so I just stayed away even though I felt something was wrong with her. She was always getting hurt. Her face was beautiful but her nose looked different. She didn't talk to anyone, which I found very strange, but why cry over spilled milk, right" My life went on; hers did too! Betty didn't even feel guilt about what she was doing to her best friend or her husband, my best friend. All we cared about was screwing our brains out. Were we both pathetic? We kept our affair from everyone I knew as soon. As Rick finds out, he'll yell and kick my ass and I will wait for it. I'm not Josh but I'm still a prick on so many levels. Betty was a man's dream come true; whatever you wanted she did it and gave it, and I was okay with that. Hiding from Rick was getting harder. She was all over my huge cock. We had no love between us, just hard core sex. She made me bang her in the back seat, on any table, on the floor, in an alley against the wall, in the park--she was a horny bunny but I kept up with her.

BROKEN DREAMS

She suck like a viper and fucked like a starving woman who need her food or a drug addict who needed her fix.

CHAPTER 10

Rick & Betty

W hat's going on, Betts? You're hiding something. You don't want sex with me. I'm going to find out. Give me some sugar, baby."

"I don't feel like having sex, Rick."

"Why not? Are you fucking someone else? Because you better tell me."

"Okay, you want to know? I'm sick and tired of being second, Rick; you're always thinking about Abby. You never got over her."

"That's not true, Betts; I married you. I love you."

"Give me a fucking break, Rick, you never loved me. It's always been Abby. Well, guess what? I'm fucking your best friend."

"What?" Rick's veins were pumping with anger. He grabs Betty and shakes her and puts her against the wall. "Who is it, Betty?"

"You're hurting me."

"I don't give a fuck, whore. Tell me--I want to hear it from your dirty mouth, bitch. I was a faithful man to you, Betts." He tightened his grip.

"Stop hurting me, Rick."

"Tell me!"

"Trevor! It's Trevor." All she could do is weep like the whore she is.

"For how long, Betty, for how long?" he shouts so loud it echoes through the walls. He truly wanted to beat the living crap out of her but he knew she was not worth going to jail for, nasty bitch that she was. "I gave you everything, Betts–with so many men, why did you have to go with my best friend Why? Answer me!" He was so angry. He took her to the bedroom. "Take your clothes off NOW!"

She does it quickly. Throwing her on the bed, I take my huge, thick cock out. "So my cock wasn't enough! Or he has a bigger dick, right?"

"Stop it."

"No! You're my wife. We are going to fuck all night, then get your fuckin' stuff out of here because I want a divorce!"

"Where do I go, Rick?"

"Go with Trevor, I don't care--just get out! You had it all, Betty. I worked hard to give you what you wanted but you like sleeping around. I never once was unfaithful, not once, so let Trevor take care of you. God knows you guys deserve each other; you both are like a snake then you bite because you can't get enough. I'm done. I can't fuck you; you make me sick. I can't stand the sight of you any longer. Get out, Betts, get out."

She scrambles for her clothes, crying like a baby.

"This is what you wanted, bitch; you're a big whore; let someone else put up with you.

Emily

The day that Josh beat me, Travis called Mom to take me to the hospital. I had a broken rib, my nose was broken again, my body ached, and my self-worth was no longer there. It was my enemy now. Why did I let my dreams get shattered in so many pieces? Why did I let myself be treated like a nobody, a hollow person with no value? Why can't he love me? Why does he still hate me for being that mean girl at school? We were young. I know he will always love Abby; that makes me weep every day. What can I do? No one is going to help me.

A nurse came in and slipped me a piece a paper. "Get help, sweetie. If your husband is beating you, all you have to do is call this number. They will help only if you want help. Fight for your life, child; he is getting away with hurting you. Don't let him."

All I could do is take the piece of paper and hold it tightly. When I got home Josh was all beaten up. My dad tried to kill him. It was a mess. The kids were so sad. Wade broke a window from across the street; he was rebelling. We had no money. My heartbreaking life was falling apart and with my depression, it was a disaster.

Time passed by slowly, if you could call it a life. Dad kept an eye on me ever since he found out I had broken bones. Mom was a lifesaver; she took the kids to school. Mom called Betts but she wouldn't come to visit me. I heard she was having some problems with Rick, probably fucking Tom, Dick and Harry. I began to be a loner. It was a lonely and dark place to be, but it was my safe place with my dark thoughts. My looks were not pretty anymore; my nose was bent from being broken so many times. When I stare at the mirror I just saw a lost woman, a broken woman with no dreams with five children. Where was that vivacious girl I used to be, full of life and exciting and attractive. Now I'm just lifeless and broken. Will I ever get out of this hellhole I made for myself? Did I deserve to be like this, worthless, sobbing, holding the sink, trying to get my wits before the kids notice? They've suffered enough. I called work to tell them I was going back to work. I ended up being a paralegal. I was close to lawyers; that was my dream but now my dreams are broken. I loved working there. They were very understanding about my life and all the time I missed. We needed money and they paid well.

Rick

I go looking for Trevor. Of course, I find him in his house drinking. I watch him from the front window. I knock. He opens the door. I punch him so hard I thought I broke my hand.

"Out of all the women you could've been with, you go with my wife. You are a back-stabbing snake. You were my best friend--why? Trevor, how could you do this to me?"

We were a bloody mess, thrashing each other until we had no more strength. I called Tommy to tell him what happened. He called Scott. Both my brothers are awesome. We meet at my place, of course. What does a man do when his heart is broken? Drink. Getting drunk with my brothers was great. Tommy is telling us about the girls he sleeps with.

"I told you, bro, she was a slut." We start to laugh.

"You always make me feel worse than when I came to see you, bro."

"You get too attached with these women; got to be like me--love them and leave them. That's my motto."

"I can't believe I came to you. Treating women like objects is not right either, like the way you're using Betty."

"Come on, bro."

We come to the conclusion that men use women and they use us; it's the way of life in some cases. "Let's go out and fuck some awesome chicks since you're single now."

"What the hell, let's do it."

We walk in a club. Tommy was wearing some slacks with his shirt opened. He looked like a pimp showing a hairy chest with his light brown hair slicked back, I just went with black slacks and white button shirt, sleeves rolled up. The music is bumping; the women are dancing and drunk. I go to the bar and have a few drinks. Turning to the dance floor I watch Tommy making a fool of himself dancing like he's stepping on a hot burning floor. His arms, up in the air, hit the woman's face. I was chucking and turning back to my drink. A beautiful woman was staring at me.

She's a red head and I prefer brunettes, but when you're hurt and down anything or any person will do. Good thing I'm not a picky man. The red head's eyes were taunting me to bang her here and now, but gentleman that I am, I will show her a good time. She's very classy; those women are the best and sexy as hell. We ended up in her house, nice and cozy; everything is cream color. The place was clean; that says a lot in my book. She puts music on and walks to me swaying her hips. She passes me a drink. I was grateful but what I really wanted was to fuck her; she knew it too. I remove her blouse to find gorgeous tits.

"Keep your glasses on; it makes you look sexy."

She nods. She smells of roses. She has a blue fitted skirt. She was so sinful removing her skirt; she had no panties and her bare pussy had a tattoo that said *Lick Me.* I smirked at her and we both had a grin a mile long.

I licked that tight pussy until she came apart. She was easy and willing. I lay on my back and she licked my shaft like a candy cane, only my cock was long, thick and flavored with sex and cream. We both enjoyed our sex fest and this was the start of something big: my addiction and drinking. You always remember your first love, your first sexual encounter, and you want more and more. I started to have my addictions. We woke up having sex again and again. I leave and go home and who do I find in my house? Betty is sitting on my sofa.

"What are you doing here, Betts?"

"Why did you beat Trevor, Rick?"

"You are unbelievable, Betts. You're a whore; get the fuck out now, or I'll throw you out."

Life is so unpredictable and yet full of surprises, so why am I miserable and lonely. I wonder about Abby. Is she happy? Is she married with kids? Is she safe? Sadness comes over my heart. She was the love of my life. That girl never realized how much she touched our lives. I truly miss her. All I could hope is that she's happy. Another day, another dollar, and another woman and another drink. I go to a bar, looking for my next pussy to fill the emptiness in my soul, even though no one can fulfill my broken heart. This was my life now; I was like a lion looking for my prey, only I hunger for a one-night stand with different cunts and my drinking was starting to escalate, but I was enjoying every minute of that life.

CHAPTER 11

Emily

A few days before Christmas, I bought a tree for my children. Mom came to help me decorate.

"Thanks Mom, it looks wonderful."

"You are beautiful, sweetie."

She hugs me and I embrace. I feel the warmth from her hug. I really needed some kind of connection. My tears run down my face. Will I be able to stop my crying someday or be happy in my own skin, or will I be a weak woman that no one will ever want? I always ask myself why me? I always wanted to fight back. My emotions are everywhere. I put some jeans on with a pink sweater, my hair in a messy bun. I'm baking a turkey and ham while Mom is wrapping the gifts for the kids.

"Need help, Mom?"

"Sure Travis, thank you, son; you've always been so helpful."

Every year we make our ornaments so you could imagine how full the tree looks. We all felt happy. Dad came a little late. We all had our dinner with no drama, thank God—well, I guess that's what I wanted to think. Josh bangs the door open and Trevor walks in with Betts. They have all been drinking. They always looked like they had a secret between them.

My dad gets up. "We're, leaving sweetheart."

I hug them with such wretchedness. I was finally feeling normal, but Josh will never be that guy who will love me forever. He always hated me; he will always love Abby. Regret is in my heart and soul. I realize now that I have to fight back and not be scared anymore, no matter what I do. I should have the power in my pathetic life. The kids went to bed.

I'm cleaning the mess in the kitchen when Trevor gets very close to me. "Merry Christmas, Em."

"Same to you, Trevor." He kisses my cheek. My body tingled. He's living with Betts.

"How have you been, Em?"

"Just dandy; can't you see tears run down my cheeks?"

He wipes them with his thumb. "What's wrong, Em?"

"Nothing. I'm just emotional right now,"

"Well, what can I do to help you?"

"Go with Betts. She's drunk. Take her home."

"We're staying the night if you don't mind."

"No, I don't mind."

"Take your hand off my wife, Trevor. Go to bed, Emmy."

"Don't tell me what to do, Josh."

"You better watch the way you talk to me,

woman."

I walk to my room being bold and with a smile. It felt great standing up for myself. Lying in my bed, I think how to plan my life because it's not working for me anymore. All I ever wanted was someone to love me, caress and make love to me, not someone that beats me because he never loved me.

Trevor & Betty

We went to a bar called Cocky Bull. I was thinking how Em looked. I'm worried about her. I've always loved that girl. Now she's a broken woman, this is my fault. She's not the same beautiful woman anymore, even though she will always be my beautiful Emily.

"Trevor, now who are you thinking of?"

"Just stop. Leave me alone for once, Betts."

"But my pussy wants your touch."

"Go find someone to fuck. You never get enough; you're like a dude." I go get a seat. I want to be alone.

Betts didn't waste any time finding someone' she's every guy's dream but I don't love her. We're friends; we go to the movies together; we go to fine restaurants; we have mind-blowing sex. My cock starts to stir but my mind is with someone else--always with someone else.

Betty gets up to sing. She has a hot pink short dress and starts singing *I'm too sexy for myself,* swaying her hips so sexy and puts her fingers through her blonde hair. Every man was whistling, yelling for her to take her clothes off. I roll my eyes; she's a slut for sure. Betts keeps dancing, picking her dress up. She's a spark in every guy's cock.

She's getting drunk, then Josh walks in. Fuck my life; he is always with a woman on his arm. He nods, going to the back room to have meaningless sex. I can't really judge him; I do the same thing but I'm not married like him, while poor Emily is home with her sadness.

Some guy takes Betts; at that moment I make a decision to leave Betty. I'd rather be alone than to be with someone who just uses men for her needs. Betts comes out of the back room with her hair a mess. She had a foursome with Josh and the two girls.

I turn around so I don't have to look at her. I'm really tired of my worthless life. I'm going to make some changes. I have been working with my dad far too long.

Betts startled me. "Take me home, Trevor." She reeked of sex. "Let's go; we have to talk at home."

I hold her arm tightly and rush her out the door. She's making me angry. We're renting a small house. It's very cozy. We walk in.

"Go take a shower; you smell like poor sex."

"Yeah, like you don't like it."

While she was taking a shower I was packing all her belongings. She comes out with my white t-shirt and no panties. She is a sexy woman but I don't love her and something has to give.

"What are you doing packing my stuff?"

"I want you to leave and please don't come back."

"Why? Trevor, we're together, baby."

"Don't touch me, Betts, We're good friends; that's it."

"I have nowhere to go."

"The way you use your pussy, you'll find a bed or a room or a cock. Just be careful."

"This is fucked up, Trevor; you're a jerk." Tears came down from her cold eyes, so I turn so I won't watch her leave.

Emily

It wasn't easy planning to leave Josh, saving a little bit of money and hiding. It was easy because he wasn't home most of the time and just didn't want to live this way any longer. It was over. Travis and Trina were living with Mom and Dad because Josh was starting to beat them. I missed them. They were in high school. I still had three to take care, even though Josh treated Wade the best. He will be the one to give me trouble about leaving his dad. A lady from work told me of a safe house where they provide counseling for me and my kids. We could stay until I find a place and get a restraining order to get Josh out of my life forever. This plan better work because this is the end for me. I can't tolerate my pitiable existence. Some days I just wanted to give up in life. I heard people say a woman that gets beaten likes it or she asks for I; that's not true. You love them and try to change them.

My phone rings. It's Betts. "Hey girl, what's up with you?"

"The same, Betts, why?"

"Have you heard Rick is with Abby, that bitch?"

"He did love her, Betts."

"Whose side are you on, Emmy?"

"Yours, but I'm not surprised he found her. Look Betts, I have my own problems."

"Well, you're not being very nice Em."

"You know what, you never asked me if I needed anything or helped with my kids. You're a selfish person, Betts. All you worry about is where your next cock is coming from, or blow job. One day, Betts, something is going to happen to you!"

"I called to tell you what's going on."

"You had him, Betty! Rick gave you everything and you threw it all away. Josh gave me heartaches and beatings. I threw my life away. Rick wasn't enough for you, so stop crying about your sorry-ass life because you lost it because you're a stupid, money-hungry woman who will never get her fill with any man. Sorry Betty, I have to go. I'm busy."

"Okay Emily, I just thought you were my friend."

"That's what I thought, Betts, until you slept with Josh."

"What are you talking about?"

"Don't insult my intelligence. Did you honestly think I didn't know the way you both stared at each other? What did you think, that I was blind? It hurt more because it was with my best friend."

"Emily, I had both of your guys!"

"What are you talking about?"

"I fucked Josh and Trevor; both cocks were in me in the same time. They were delicious. You could never handle both of those cocks; that's why they came to me."

"You're a whore, Betty. Don't ever call me again."

I don't know why I'm crying. I knew she was fucking them--what a slut! She wonders why no one cares about her--how could any guy stay with a tramp like her?

Focus on the plan, Emily. Talking to myself, I get all my money together, put it in a bag, get my children and our clothes together, and stuff them in bag really quick. I call the lady; she tells me to wait in a gas station. I was trembling something awful. I'm almost there, my freedom. I could feel my heart beating like I was running a marathon. My tears run down my face; I want to be free so badly, when I hear the door slam.

"Where are you, bitch?"

Oh my God, Josh is home. The lady is waiting for me. Oh God, please! Let me be free; give me my freedom. I'll never ask for anything else; I just want a better life for me and my kids.

"Why don't you answer me?"

"I was putting the clothes away."

He grabs me. "I want some sex."

"I have to pick the kids from school."

"They can wait."

"NO!! They can't wait. Go fuck Betty."

"What you did you say?"

"Yeah, I know about you and Trevor having a threesome; she told me, Josh."

He pushes me hard on the wall. "I'm going to fuck you hard."

"NO!"

He pulls my hair, slapping me like a rag doll. Lying on the bed, I don't let him touch me. I slap Josh on the face.

"You shouldn't have done that."

He starts beating me. He leaves me on the bed with a puddle of blood all over the bed. It looks like out of a scary movie. When I wake up, still on the bed, I grab all the sheets and put them in a bag. I'm taking a shower when I hear Trevor call my name.

"Emily, are you ok?"

"I want to be alone, please."

He never listens. He sees me sobbing on the tile floor while the water streams down my body.

"Hey, baby girl."

"Go away!" My sobs get worse.

Trevor picks me up and dries me with a towel. He is staring at me. "He hit you, Em?"

All I do is cry, tears streaming down my face. My body is wounded. I feel like hell. My bruises were swelling up. Every inch of my body was in agony. My body can't take any more injuries. Haven't I suffered enough? Asking myself these questions isn't helping. All Trevor could do is hold me and comfort me. I could feel his anger. He finished dressing me with such gentleness, something I haven't felt in so long, and I let him. He made something to eat. I fell asleep for a couple hours. He gave me some aspirin to ease my aching body.

CHAPTER 12

Emily

Time passed by so quickly. I heard Abby left Rick and Betts went running to him, then he kicked her out because she was using him--all this drama between them. My life spiraled to a road of destruction. I was still planning to leave Josh; that was my mission in life. He is a monster in disguise of cuteness, but the reality he was a man with no feelings, no love–just an empty shell. I'm getting ready for Betty's funeral. She killed herself. I felt badly because I never talked to her after that day when she told me she slept with Josh and Trevor. Someone raped her. She couldn't live with that. Who could blame her? I felt the same when I got raped.

The skies seem angry, with gray clouds. It was a heartrending day for all of us. We were in the church and Josh was saying things to Rick about Betty. He embarrassed me and her poor parents. I got up and left. Rick was beating Josh and truth be told, I was happy let him feel what he did to me for years.

I call the lady from the safe house. I pick up my three children; of course, they're not happy. Wade was always giving me problems but I was determined to change my life and not even my kids will change my mind. It was hard the first few days. We had meetings with all the women who had been beaten and heard their poignant stories. We were all depressed; that was the part of healing. It was my turn to tell the ladies about my gloomy life. I was so nervous and I started with when I was six, the mean girl in school, then when I married Josh, when he started to beat me--I wasn't proud of what happened in my life to be telling strangers how pathetic my life was with the beatings getting worse. So many years wasted--my tears flowed down my cheeks.

"I thought I was going to change him but I never did. He broke my nose three times, my arms, my ribs—I had to lie to my family and friends for the guilt and embarrassment. I never had a good day; my kids were always scared. I felt like a horrible mother every day but I always said I would change him. One day I went out with my friend to a bar because just I wanted to have fun but when I walked in didn't want to be there, so I ran out of the old bar. I don't know why; I just ran out and the unthinkable happened: a guy with a mask grabs me…" At this point I am weeping. I take a deep breath. "Sorry." Kelly tells me to take my time. "He had a knife on my neck. He raped me; I couldn't stop him." I fall to my knees, covering my face with a quilt. "And sadness at what happened that night changed me forever." Kelly hugs me and I lean my head on her chest. "I was broken, my faith was gone, my dreams were shattered and all I could do is cry for what seemed like forever, but I always said to myself I'm still alive."

I was getting stronger every day at the safe house. Learning to love myself was the toughest thing. I haven't loved myself for a long time. My self-esteem was near-gone. I had to get better. No one would never hit or abuse me ever again. Enough is enough; the kids are in their teens. It's hard for them to be here. They had counseling and are calm for now. I was praying to God that we would get through this insanity. The next morning I was helping the women cleaning after breakfast. Kelly asked for me to go to her office. When I walked in she said, "Have a seat, Emily."

I sat on a comfy sofa. "I wanted to talk to you, Emily, about you going to school, for you could be a social worker or counselor; you could help other women."

"I would love to do that, Kelly."

Kelly helped me get an apartment and gave me a grant to go college. Josh still didn't know where we were so we felt safe. Feeling normal was amazing. I kept finding myself smiling and singing. Months passed. I was a new person, stronger. I had friends from the safe house. My life was coming together. It was my turn to be happy. I don't even want a man because my happiness is so real and I don't want that feeling to ever leave my heart and soul.

My graduation was today. I bought a beautiful dress at the Goodwill. It was cheap but who would care anyway? Afterward, my friends threw me a little party. We were having such a good time when they surprised me--my mom and dad, Travis and Trina. I couldn't stop sobbing. I held my children so tightly. Eighteen and twenty, they were going to move to Arizona to go to college. I was so proud of them. My dad established their living arrangements. My parents helped me every step of the way. I was so grateful. I became a counselor at the safe house and was so happy to help other women to stop them from the beatings. Saturday was sunny and the skies were blue. It was a beautiful day. I felt beautiful going to Tracy's café. Waiting in line a voice whispers in my ear, "Try the blueberry muffins; they're to die for."

"Did I ask you for your opinion?"

"No sweetie, I just wanted to let you know what was best here."

"I'm not your sweetie, ok?"

"Sure, beautiful."

I roll my eyes. *Is he for real?* is all I could think.

"My name is John Bloom, if you were wondering."

"I wasn't wondering. If your last name is Bloom…"

"Be nice, beautiful."

I couldn't stop giggling.

"Let me buy you dinner."

"I don't know you!"

"Please stop breaking my heart."

I stare at him. He's cute: green eyes, medium brown hair, tall, tan like me, full lips. It's been so long since I've been with a man. I say yes. It's too soon but I ask myself when do I start living? I'm ready. No one is ever going beat me or treat me like I'm not worthy because if I learned anything it is that I'm worth it and I deserve to be loved.

Getting dressed for my date, I'm wearing a pink dress, some light pink heels and my dark brown hair flowing down my shoulder. With my tan skin it was tough looking in the mirror. My nose is a bit crooked. I'm very self-conscious. I'm not young anymore; all I have is lots of regrets. It's time to start a normal life. It's what I wish for, and I will fight for it with every ounce of my being. I'm not weak anymore. Josh broke me more than once. It's not okay. I lift my head up high, feeling giddy like a young girl, with butterflies in my stomach. It is the best emotion, like a school girl. Mom took the kid to Disneyland so I could go on this date. I'm meeting

John at Tracy's café because I don't want him to know where I live. I get out of the car. He has a beautiful smile. He makes me smile. I almost forgot what this felt like.

"Hi beautiful."

"Hi John."

"Are you ready?"

"Yes, you're lovely."

"Thank you."

John opens the door of his sports car door for me. He takes me to a five-star restaurant. All he does is smile at me, a sweet nice smile. "I'm so nervous!"

"Don't be."

We drink white wine.

"So Emily, tell me about yourself. I want the truth and lots of dates; don't tell me lies."

"Okay John, I have five children, I was married to a guy who beat me, and I'm now a counselor for battered woman in a halfway house."

"Wow! Don't hold back now, beautiful."

"My life has been a train wreck. I just want some peace in my life."

"I don't blame you, Emily. It seems you've gone through so much!"

"I have. It's been a long time. This is really nice. Enough about me--what about you, John?"

"I've been married once. I have a five-year-old little girl named Jill Bloom, my little angel. My wife passed two years ago of cancer. So I'm a single dad." He has a poignant smile again.

"My five children are good; they've gone through so much with Josh. He was a very violent person. He was unfaithful and the worst dad. I always felt guilty for what I let them see what in our home."

John nods his head. We went for a walk for a while. This was the best date I ever had. He was so gentle with the way he holds my hands. This was blissful and wonderful.

CHAPTER 13

Emily & John

Two months passed. John and I are like boyfriend and girlfriend. The feeling was so normal and lovely. We're going Santa Barbara for the weekend. We haven't had sex yet! I just wanted to be sure--so many mistakes in my past, so much hurt and disappointment and regret. I want my second chance to be breathtaking. John takes my breath away in such a brilliant way. I guess it's true: when you no longer love someone the doors open to so much possibility. It's like the shield comes down. Love was blind when it came to Josh. John was my surprise because truth be told, I wasn't looking for anyone. He's smart and caring; he loves his daughter; he is a lawyer--he's perfect, but I know all too well no man is perfect.

I hear the knock at the door and practically run to the door. When I open it all I can see is a gorgeous man in front of me. His green eyes sparkle. His brown hair is messy and he's wearing jeans and a white t-shirt. He works out--nice muscles. I'm just gawking at him, poor guy.

"Hi beautiful."

"Hi John, ready?"

"Absolutely ready--by the way, you look lovely, Emily."

My face feels warm. "I'm just wearing jeans and a black sweater, John."

"You look good in them--more than good, fantastic." He holds me and kisses me with so much passion. We walk to the car. To my surprise, it's a motor home. "I thought I wanted you to myself."

BROKEN DREAMS

We run to get on our way, holding hands. We are in front of the beach. It's beautiful. All we could hear is the waves. There's a chill but I welcome the breeze on my face. John holds me and kisses my neck. "I can't wait to love you, Emily."

I turn to him. My tears flow down my cheeks. We stare at each other; he slides his large hands, holding my face. The waves from the beach sound wonderful. He kisses me with such longing; our tongues swirl. It was gentle, with so much passion and lust. John carries me inside and lays me down on the bed. It is candle-lit, so romantic, with so many roses. It's lovely that he took the time for me. No one ever has done this for me. I bite my lip with anticipation.

"Do you want me, beautiful, as much as I want you?"

"Yes John, I really do!"

He removes my jeans so slowly his fingers make me tingle with the feel of such a simple act. He kisses my toes, my legs--I'm so wet for him. He opens the lips of my pussy. When his tongue licks the inner walls, I almost fall apart. He spreads my legs apart more. I bite my bottom lip. I yell, "John, please, I'm going to come!"

"Do you want me to stop, beautiful?"

"NO!! Don't stop."

He puts my legs on his shoulders for more access to my bare pussy. John stops and smiles, kissing my stomach. He starts to suck my breasts, playing with them. At this point I'm so horny. His breath is warm on my skin. It's been so long for me. He finally shows me his massive cock. How this man is gifted; I can't wait to lick and suck that perfect monstrous cock.

John was so good at making me wait; the sensation was amazing. He toyed with me every chance he got, loving every touch, lick and suck was wonderful. John slides in my bare pussy. I felt full of the love of a man who treated me like a woman, a man who knew how to love. He had passion, lust, and romance. He pushes in and out to the tip so slow, I close my eyes--it was too much. I am squeezing the sheets for dear life. We both have intense orgasms.

"Oh! Oh John!"

He is gifting me with kisses on my face, neck, hair and shoulders. When I open my eyes our tongues meet with such want and hunger. We sleep holding each other. What a serene feeling. I never wanted this night to end but I know all too well everything ends one way or another. I wake up nude with the sound of waves splashing the rocks and a hunk of a man by my side. Life is good. He wakes with a grin. I smile with such contentment. John's finger traces my cheeks to my lips. We started to kiss. We didn't care about morning breath. Our tongues connected with such passion. He feels my breast. I kiss his mouth and neck, going down, kissing his abs; his huge shaft enlarges. My mouth opens wide and I moan. He tastes sweet; his smell is all man. I start sucking. He took hold of my hair, pushing his cock down my throat. All his cum flows down my throat. I swallow quickly. He brings me to his mouth. We kiss deeply. He lays me down facing him. He spreads my legs and licks my wet pussy, teasing me. It felt wonderful opening my legs to a man who wanted me and only me. I gasped at this amazing feeling. I arch my back and wrap my legs around his neck.

"You taste divine, beautiful. I want to eat you all day, Emily." And with that I come with an intense orgasm.

John and I watch the waves--what a beautiful sight. This is heaven. We are drinking coffee; the air has a chill but I welcome it with a real man who wants me for me. I know when I get back I'm going to have to face Josh and Trevor; it's been a year. I just love these wonderful emotions. We go for a walk. John makes dinner. He's a fine cook. This man is perfect and he's mine. We spend the weekend making love, going to the beach and walking. We didn't want to go back to the real life but we had our responsibilities and our children, so we have to go back to reality. Our weekend is over and with sadness we go back to reality of our lives.

Josh & Trevor

"When I find that bitch I'm going to beat the shit out of her."

"Shut up, Josh; you're not going to touch her anymore, so stop being an asshole."

We're getting drunk. Ever since Emily left we've been drinking. I miss her. I know now I've been in love with her all these years. Josh treated her so badly. I didn't save her. I'm going to tell her how I feel. Josh is my friend but if he hits her again I'm going to beat him down. She's always been mine. I'll fight for her. She will not be with other guys because I'm that guy. She won't want a drunk. I've got to put my life together. She'll be back soon; I've got to be ready. Josh has been drinking, doing drugs, fucking random women--he's a big mess. What am I talking about? We're a huge mess. I call Rick to go to an AA meeting with him. We used to be best friends but not any longer. He was surprised I wanted help. He won't deny anyone help. He's an author now and married. He's so happy he finally got over Abby. Now I know what he feels. I love Emily. Josh is going downhill. It's amazing how he's still working with his lifestyle. We don't have sex with other women together. He was getting girls from the street and doing drugs; he didn't care about venereal diseases. I wasn't going that road.

Josh yells and pushes the woman that's next to him snoring. "What the fuck? Get out! You're not letting me sleep, stupid whore; get out!"

"Stop pushing me, asshole; you get what you want and you treat me like dirt."

"Yeah, yeah, tell someone who gives a fuck."

The woman leaves and slams the door on the way out. I go back to sleep. Hours pass. It's raining so badly and making my mood get even worse. Where the fuck is Trevor? I didn't realize it's been three days of just fucking women and doing drugs and sleep. I take a shower and try to eat something, thinking Emily can't hide forever. When I get my hands on her I'm going to kick her ass. No one keeps my kids away from me or gets away from me, that stupid bitch!! I'll show her who's boss, then I'm going to bang her senseless. I can't wait to see her. I'm going to set her straight.

Trevor goes to see Josh knocking on the door. He opens it. He's drinking again. I guess he's feeling sorry for himself. "Hey dude, what's up? Let's go to Cocky Bull."

"I've been going to AA meetings."

"You will never stop drinking or fucking sluts, Trevor; you love that life as much as I do!"

"Well, I'm going to try anyway."

"Whatever. I got some news: I heard that Emily is coming back but not to live. She's not going to hide anymore."

"Well, that's great news. I can't wait to see her and my son Wade."

"You have five kids, not one, Josh!"

"I don't feel those are my children."

"You're an asshole. No wonder Emily left."

"Leave so I can go to Cocky Bull."

"I came to ask you to come to one meeting."

"Fuck no, never, Trevor."

I just walked out. Damn loser.

Emily

When I got back from my wonderful weekend with John, I realized my life was getting much improved and nothing was going to alter that! I won't let that happen.

I could still feel John's hands on me and my whole body fires up. Oh my! I wish could call him so he could make sweet love to me. Taking a shower, washing my body, soap sliding down my body, feeling myself, my moans are low thinking its John's finger in my sweet spot. My orgasm is intense.

The time has come to face Josh. All I could hope is he leaves me alone forever. Working taking phone calls for abused women could be exhausting. You'd be surprised how many women get abused. I know all too well how they feel. Some 85 percent of domestic abuse victims are women; 15 percent are men. It's very heartbreaking. The number of American women who are murdered by current or ex male partners during that time was 11,766. That's nearly double the amount of casualties. John calls and my heart skips a beat.

"Hi sweetie."

"Hello beautiful, would you like to go to lunch with me?"

"Of course."

"I'll pick you up. I can't wait to see you."

"So Mister Bloom, you're missing me?"

"Don't tease me, beautiful; I'll punish you."

"Oh, please do!"

"Know my shaft is growing hefty for you."

We both laugh. "See you later, okay?"

John takes me to his house. The table is full of food. He carries me in the bedroom. He touches my cheek.

"I've missed you."

I smile. Our tongues are dancing with the beat of our hearts. He removes my clothes. Being nude in front of him, I feel powerful. He gets on his knees, licking my legs. I sit on the edge of the bed, my thighs open brazenly for him. Still on his knees, he licks my vagina like he couldn't get enough of me. I pull his hair for more; my appetite is yearning for him. The feeling of passion was too much.

"Please John, more baby, more, don't stop, please don't stop!"

He stops with a huge grin and pulls me on top. Riding this man was a pleasure. As he squeezes my nipples, bouncing up and down, our climax subsides. We hold each other, giving sweet kisses.

"I love you, Emily. I want you every day for the rest of my life."

"I love you too, John."

We had to eat and go back to work. All I wanted to do was stay in bed with this awesome man but we can't, so I treasure my minutes, hours and days with John. John doesn't want me to see Josh. He's scared he'll kill me once and for all. I have to start fresh--no more hiding.

CHAPTER 14

Emily & Josh

The day has come to face Josh and my demons. I'm no longer that stupid or weak woman that he broke or took my dreams away. Now they're just broken dreams. I put yoga pants, t-shirt and a jacket, just in case he tries something. My heart is beating a mile an hour but not from being scared. I'm not scared to die; sometimes I would have welcomed it when I was with Josh. Now I want to live because finding John was a blessing and my children--how loving them made the most awful moments seem less. When staring in the mirror I don't see that broken woman anymore; I see a strong warrior, a brave woman. I could stand in front of anything or anyone. Putting my hair up in a bun, I walk to my car to go to the house where Josh is staying. I knock on the door, my hand firm. I can't show weakness. He opens the door. He's in shock–well, we both are. He's full of tattoos. Josh has always been gorgeous; now he has muscles. He surprises me by pushing me inside.

"Well, well, bitch, you finally show your face." He pulls my hair. I could hear the pouring rain. I can't let him beat me. I kicked him on the groin. He yelled.

"Josh, you will never hit me again, loser."

"I'm going to kill you, bitch!"

"Do it! I don't care anymore, Josh."

He gets up and runs for me. I open the door. It's pouring. I run outside in the dark. He grabs my arm and hits me in the face. I fall in the ground. We're rolling, hitting each other. Of course, no one helps. Rain-soaked, I kick him; he gets on top of me. I have no escape. He's got me; he's going to kill me. He slaps my face a few times. With the pressure of his body I can't get up.

"What did you think, Emmy, that you were going to make me look like a fool or beat me like that movie *Enough* with Jennifer Lopez? No bitch, I'm going to carry you inside and fuck your brains out, then I'm going to kill you, or maybe kill us both--that would be poetic justice, so people will remember us, bitch."

He was holding me firmly. Tears fell down my cheeks with the falling rain. He lifted me up, pulling my hair. Oh my God, it hurt so badly. I hear a voice.

"Let her go, Josh or I'll kill you!"

"Get the fuck out of here, Trevor; she's not yours."

Trevor pushes Josh and they start fighting. I'm just standing in the rain, brokenhearted. Once best friends, now enemies, they were bleeding. I could feel my cheek and eyes swell up. Trevor leaves Josh on the ground; he carries me to his car and calls the police.

BROKEN DREAMS

After talking to the police, they took Josh to jail where he belongs. Trevor took me to his house. The house was nice and comfy, like a bachelor pad. My face was hurting; my legs were scraped. He carries me into the shower. I'm numb. I don't know why I'm letting him; maybe I'm just tired of it all. I could hear the storm outside, hitting the windows. Trevor doesn't say a word; he's removing every piece of my clothing. They're soaked. The warm water hits my sore body; all of a sudden a warm naked body is holding me.

"What are you doing, Trevor?"

He puts his finger on my mouth to silence me. I stayed silent but this feels wrong. I'm with John and he will never forgive me. Trevor kisses my neck. I turn to see him. He has so many tattoos, and his muscles are larger than Josh's. He's not a boy anymore; he's a beautiful man. When I stare at Trevor's eyes, there's an unhappiness and sadness. He speaks. "Let me love you, Em. I want you so badly it hurts."

"It's wrong, Trevor. I have a boyfriend."

"He won't know. Let me feel that lovely body of yours, please. I've wanted you for so long." Trevor kisses me like he's a starving man. He kisses me like there's no tomorrow. It's making me so horny. It's wrong but I can't help myself. The water is pouring like we're under a waterfall. He sucks on my tits roughly. Yeah! It feels so damn good. He pulls my hair and our tongues reunite like in the past. It's familiar and yet new. Licking my neck and back, sucking on my nipples-hunger ignites to my core. It's all we could feel; our bodies are on fire. Trevor scoops me up in his arms. We're so wet; all the drops are falling on the floor. He gently lays me on the bed. He stares at me.

"I've waited so long for this, Em." He licks his lips with eagerness.

I bite my bottom lip. He opens my legs and starts to lick my sweet spot.

"Oh! Ahhh! Trevor more, more please!"

He licks with no mercy. I love it all of it.

"YES! Yes!"

BROKEN DREAMS

His tongue does his magic and my orgasm is so intense. He lies down and puts me on top, watching me. I ride him as he touches my breasts. Putting my head back, the amazing ride of his cock is huge and he hits my G-spot quick and I bounce harder and we come together. I must look like a monster. Trevor gets a towel to clean my pussy. He holds me securely as only a man could and I welcome his embrace. We kiss and stare at each other for a moment until we fall sound asleep.

I wake up in the arms of the wrong man. My life could never be simple and my head is aching. Trevor is sound asleep. What have I done? With aches and soreness all over my body and so much regret, I know John is worried about me. He's going to hate me. He'll never forgive me for being unfaithful. I go take a shower,putting on the same clothes. Trevor stares at me.

"Where are you going, Em?"

"To my boyfriend, Trevor! What we did was wrong."

"Don't go, Em. I love you. I've always loved you, Em."

"What do you mean you always loved me?"

"Em, I was scared to tell you when we first slept together. I knew then I wanted you forever!"

I was in shock at what he was confessing. "Why tell me now?"

He walks to me, holding my shoulders. "I was a fool, Em. I knew you loved Josh and that you couldn't possibly love me." Tears stream down his face.

"You knew he was beating me."

"I never knew what Josh was doing to you. I always knew he was mean to you, but not beating you, I swear." Trevor hugs me like he never wanted to let go.

"I'm sorry, I have to go. It's too late for us."

"Don't say that, Emily. Please just think about it."

"There is nothing to think about. You and Josh were man whores, sleeping around. You could've fought for me but you didn't."

He sobs, holding me firmly. "Please, Em, you were not mine. You married him; what did you expect me to do--be a monk while you loved and were living with Josh? I tried to be there for you. I treasured the time we had, but I knew you would never leave him."

"I kept a secret from you, Trevor. Travis and Trina are your children."

"What are you saying, Em? Mine?"

"Yes, they're yours. Josh treated them badly and never connected with them because he knew they weren't his."

"Why didn't you tell me? Why keep something so important from me?"

"They only look like you, Trevor. You loved your life and you chose to ignore this fact. I had to send them with my mom and dad because Josh started to hit them. He hated them. He stayed with me because he didn't want us to be happy. I have to go and face John and hope he forgives me."

"If you love him, Em, don't tell him."

"I have to; I'm not going to lie." My own tears flowed down my cheeks.

We hugged each other.

"I want you so much, Em; please consider that we could be happy and tell my children that I'm their dad."

"They're adults now, Trevor. I made a mess in all our lives because I thought one day Josh would change and love me. He never did because his love was Abby."

I walked out of Trevor's home with regrets, sadness and overwhelming pain in my heart that he always loved me and never told me. If he had told me, my life could've been different. I go home with my swollen face and throbbing body--even my pussy was tender. How many times did we have sex last night? John left so many messages on my recorder. His voice was frantic. All I wanted was to be alone for hours, drinking hot tea and waiting for when John comes to my house for answers. I put so on much make-up to hide the bruises that I looked like a clown, turn on the television watching *Bridget Jones* and singing, "All by myself! I want to be all by myself!" Tears fall with my emotions. What I am going to do? Confusion overwhelms me. My heart is crushed. I utterly want to die. Making a mess of my life! I'm just a broken mess with broken dreams. Once I've calmed down I take deep breath. I'm always thinking of what my life has been. I always thought I would be a lawyer and I would marry and have a great life. Those dreams vanished the minute I went with Josh. I can't keep weeping over what could've been; it's what I do with my life here and now–that's right; there's always tomorrow. Well, that's what I keep telling myself. Life sucks on so many levels but life goes on with devastating broken pieces of a broken heart with broken dreams and so many regrets.

CHAPTER 15

Emily & John

I fell asleep at some point on the sofa watching a movie. There's a knock at the door, waking me up. I open the door to see an angry face. It's John. His jaw falls when he sees my face. "What the fuck happened to you, Emily? Please don't tell me that Josh did this to you because I'm going to kill that piece of shit!" He runs to me and holds me gently so my body won't ache. More tears fall like an out of control faucet that won't turn off. I let him hold me because truth be told, when I confess my shameless, unfaithful deeds I did to a wonderful man, he will hate me forever. John lifts my chin to take a good look at my injuries. His jaw twitches in anger.

"Is that bastard in jail?"

"Yes!"

"Where you, Emily?"

I swallowed hard. This is when I lose my friend, the love of my life, and for what? For a lustful rumble in bed with someone who was a man whore that kept his secret that he loved me and never told me.

"Answer me, Emily!"

I stare at his gorgeous, flawless face, biting my bottom lip. "Could we have a seat?"

We walk to the sofa. I take a deep breath, my lips trembling, tears flowing down my cheeks. "What's wrong, Emily?"

"I was with Trevor at his house; he saved me from Josh."

John smiles. "I wish it was me that was saving you." His smile turns sad. "I'm glad he was there. So you know him?"

"Yes, he was a friend from school."

"You could've called me, Emily."

"I was hurt and confused and so distraught I couldn't think straight."

"What are you trying to say?"

"I slept with Trevor and my first two children are his."

John gets up so quickly he frightens me. "I was worried about you and you were busy fucking your ex-lover? What a fool I must look to you."

I look down, feeling ashamed of what I did to an amazing man. He grabs me to take a good look at my face. "I want you to take a good look for the last time, Emily; I would've given you the whole world. I loved you so much and what do you do? You shatter my heart, you unfaithful bitch. I got what I deserved to love a woman with broken dreams and a broken heart, someone who didn't love me. I thought you loved me, Emily; how could you do this to me? I wish you the best, Emily."

All I could do is weep. He was leaving me. He stared at me once more. His tears were sliding down his face. "No woman has ever made me cry." Shaking his head, he runs out of my house. The house was very silent and I fell to the floor sobbing, with my broken dreams all over the floor along with my heart and tears.

Emily

Days passed. I was working and didn't speak with anyone. I went home got some wine and sat on the sofa weeping with all my regrets and the wretchedness of my tormented life. It's entirely my fault. Trevor leaving messages was getting me sick to my stomach. I never want to see him again. Going out with the girls at Cocky Bull--I haven't been there since I was raped. I won't leave the girlfriends; they know not to leave me alone. My friends had been to hell and back. Our life was just having kids and getting beaten up for years; now we were strong woman who never let any man hit us, ever. Cocky Bull's music was rocking. I started swaying my hips with my BFFs Paige, Liza and Tiffany. All our children are adults; we could do what we want. I could see Tommy is coming our way, the man-whore of all time. Paige's blue eyes light up.

"Don't do it, Paige. He's Rick's brother and a player. He uses women."

Paige laughs. "How about that? I want to use him, too."

"Well, I warned you, my good friend."

"Would you beautiful ladies love a drink?"

We all say yes at the same time. He smirks. His eyes didn't leave Paige's body. She does have a lovely body: her breasts are large, and she has fair skin and long straight hair, a small figure with heart hips, and crystal blue eyes. I was watching them. I hope he won't hurt her. I turn and who do I see? John with a date; he was dancing. With my tears falling I turn around and ask for a shot because I wanted to be numb with my own misery. My heart was broken and this makes it worse. Tiffany comes to keep me company.

"Take it easy there, sister."

John eyes just watch me. Some guy came to ask me to dance I say, "No, thank you."

He didn't like that. He grabbed my arm. "You're a friggin' tease." He was drunk. Someone socked him in the jaw.

"When a woman says no she means no, asshole. What are you doing here, Emily?"

"I could ask you the same. You can't tell me what to do, John, and your date looks pretty angry." His date huffs and walks out. He runs after her. My sadness is back with a vengeance. He did show he cares about me; he just hates me right now. Drinking some more, I'm drunk. Someone taps my shoulder. I turn thinking it is John but no, surprise! It's Trevor.

"I'm going to take you home."

"How did you know I was here? Are you stalking me?"

"So what Em, I love you. I don't want something to happen to you!"

"Fuck you! I don't want anything to do with you!"

Trevor's face turns to a sadness I've never seen before. "Let me take you home, Em."

All I could do is shake my head.

Emily & Trevor

Trevor takes me to his home. I was drunk. He carries me to his bed. I start to cry. He kisses my tears away.

"Don't cry, baby girl; everything will be all right!"

My tears fall on the soft pillow. With his fingers he slides my hair away from my face. He gives me tender kisses, his long, thick tongue licking my cheeks and down my neck. He sucks my nipple so softly. I moan. What a feeling! His heartbeat is fast; his tongue is sliding to my sweet spot.

"I'm going to make you feel better, woman." I open my thighs with no shame; of course, I'm drunk but the sensation was out of this world. Damn the consequences of tomorrow. "Don't cry, baby. I'm here to rock your world whenever you need me. You were meant for me, Emily."

I was holding her while she sleeps. She's beautiful but I could see the damage what Josh did to her. Her nose is not the same. I wish now I could've saved her; now she's broken and a very strong woman indeed. I've always loved her and always will, taking what I could get from her even if she hates me. She is the mother of my children. Tear flows down my face. She saved them by letting her mom take them. That must've been so tough for her as a mother missing them so much. My Travis and Trina don't know I'm their father. Will they ever respect me or hate me?

Well, I'll soon find out. Sound asleep, she stirs and reality kicks me in the ass the way she looks at me, with regret.

"Taking advantage of a drunken woman is not your style, or maybe it is!"

"Don't blame me that you wanted me, Em. I love you!"

"Just be quiet, Trevor. I hate you, Trevor! I hate you!"

"Why are you doing this Em?"

"I was drunk, not knowing what I was doing."

"You were yelling give me more, baby, moaning and wanting more."

"Shut the fuck up, Trevor! I've got a headache! All I'm doing is making more mistakes." He tries to touch me. It felt like acid burning my skin.

"Em, stop treating me like this."

"Just don't touch me ever again and when you see me, don't talk to me, please." I get up, get dressed and I leave him. Trevor stays in bed in shock.

CHAPTER 16

Emily

I'm like a robot, just functioning with my regrets and struggling with my mistakes. I start to clean my house with tears. Paige comes to help me with a bottle of wine. We're sitting on the sofa.

"What's up with you, Paige? Are you still seeing Tommy the man-whore?"

"Well, he's not that bad."

"You like him?"

She smiles.

"I know that smile, girl. He's good in bed; he

makes me peanut butter and jelly sandwiches for breakfast. She giggles. *That's weird,* I thought.

"So he's always horny too; all guys are horny. He gets me really hot. He knows what buttons to push, We're just a hot, nasty mess." We couldn't stop laughing.

"Well, as long he treats you well, that's what matters." We stand and start dancing The Pointer Sisters. "He's so shy… We sway our asses, yelling, "He's so shy; I'll love him to the day I die. Oh yeah!"

We giggle, pouring some more wine. We get sad and fall asleep.

I go see my mom. She has my breakfast ready. "Hi mom." Hugging my mom is so amazing. I love her dearly; she has been my rock through thick and thin. We talk; of course, she asks if there's a man in my life. I couldn't tell her what a mess my life is so I tell her, "No, I don't need anyone, Mom--just my family."

I drive around watching couples walking their kids and dogs. I smile. I never had a dog. I always wanted one I go to a dog shelter. It smells of all the dogs caged up. Feeling like them at one time in my life, I walk through slowly. Their eyes are so gloomy, asking for help. One gets my attention. He looks like a snow ball only he's dirty. He has one brown eye and a blue. He is so cute. I want him. When I carry him he licks my face. He makes me happy. I want to save him like someone saved me. I put him down.

"I'll take him."

My day was spent putting a doggy door in my back door, then I go buy toys, dog food and blankets. I realized dogs love you unconditionally, even when you're not perfect. All you have to do is give your heart and they give their love and heart--such beautiful creatures.

When I come home from work, Snowball runs to me like he was missing me so much! The feeling is amazing. I let him lick my face. We both show our love for each other. He made my day beautiful.

John calls me to tell me Josh got two years for

trying to kill me. John was the prosecutor at the trial. They were letting him go. He fought so they would at least keep him in jail.

"Thank you, John, for all your help."

"Anytime, Emily. Take care of yourself."

"You too." Sadness creeps in my heart at the love that got away. Snowball licking my toes makes me smile, so I'm kissing my cute Shih Tzu and bathing him. "I bought you a new sweater. I hope you like it. Dog clothing is expensive." I started walking with Snowball. He loves to walk My next-door neighbor is wearing a tight t-shirt showing his gut and his underwear, with a cigar in his mouth.

"Hi baby cakes, you're looking fine these days."

"Thanks Gray.

He winks at me every time. Yuck! I walk fast to my destination. Seven-eleven has the best coffee and it's cheap. "Come on, Snowball. do your business." Walking back home, thank God Gray went inside. He always looks at me as if I was nude.

Well, the house is clean now. What do I do with no life. But I love my life—it's maybe a little lonely. I run to that dark place at times with no man but that's okay. I can live with that, It's more a problem having a man anyway.

Josh

Get me out, Dad! Fuck that bitch; she filed charges and now they gave me two years, Dad!"

"Two years? Well son, you deserved it. You should never hit a woman, especially the mother of your children. Don't cry to me again. You're just a loser, Josh. Grow up, son. Sorry, but you need tough love, son. You're too old for this kind of behavior. Do the two years, Josh. Maybe that's what you need. Sorry, don't call me again until you change your life."

"I don't need your fuckin' advice, asshole. He hung up on me. Fuck you. Fuck all of you."

Josh ends up in the hole for a month for disrespect.

Josh

Sitting in my jail cell was driving me crazy. That bitch-what does she think, that she's the boss? I should've killed her for what she's done. All we do here is think. I haven't thought about Abby for such a long time. I actually dream about her and when I used to kiss her sweet, full lips. When she held my face with her soft hands, she was an amazing girl, and now she's a beautiful woman. I always wonder what if we had stayed together. I miss her charm and innocence. I truly loved that girl, the one that got away. Why Kyle? Why did you leave me when I needed you the most! I became a monster, a woman beater! Fucking every pussy I could stick my dick in; Mom and Dad hate me; I never see them and now they won't help me. I'm caged like an animal with no pussy or drugs and no one to beat. I haven't seen my kids. I'm going to kill Trevor for beating my ass. It was true; I stayed with Emily so Trevor wouldn't have her. Yeah, I'm an asshole… two years in this hellhole. Guys staring at me, probably trying to tap my ass. I'll kill whoever tries for sure. All I do all day is read. Life sucks. I dream of a beautiful girl, curls bouncing while she runs to me with her short jean shorts and her smile that would make me throw her on the ground and kiss her sweet red lips. Her hazel eyes sparkle. She plays with my jet-black hair. Mercy, she made my dick stir to life. She doesn't know this because she's too innocent. When her finger slides down my lips I suck it. I'm getting hot. Waking up all I see is cement walls and my cock standing so I start jacking off until my cum is all over my hand. I'm getting pissed. I don't want to be here.

The guards take me to eat. The food is gross. I take

my tray of food with every guy looking where I'm going to sit. Hideous fuckers…sitting with the nerds is my best bet. Before I could have a seat some dude started to beat me. One starts to stab me on my arms and legs. Thank God the knife is small. Blood is all over the place. All I start to see is stars. One guy said. "We don't like woman beaters." When I awake the doctor is talking to the nurse, giving me drugs. I go into a deep sleep, wishing that Kyle would come for me. I guess time will heal my wounds. They will put me in my own cell. Word got around that I'm in for domestic violence. They were going to kill me.

Tommy & Paige

"I asked you to dinner, Paige, because I wanted to ask to move in together."

Paige could not believe what she was hearing; she

spit all her wine. "We can't, Tommy; what we have is just sexual."

"No baby, it's not. The day I met you knew I was in trouble. You bring the best out of me. I've never been in love with anyone." I hold her hand because for the first time I'm scared of losing someone I want so badly. "Please just think about it!"

"There's nothing to think about, Tommy. I don't want a man who loves to go with so many women. You're known as a man-whore."

"I would never do that with you Paige. I love you. I fell hard for you, baby. Please think about it?"

We eat our dinner. My stomach is all twisted. I feel like I'm going to lose Paige and the food I'm digesting. I never thought in my wildest dreams I would fall in love with anyone. When I told Rick he started to laugh at me. I know now how he felt about the love of his life; that was Abby. I always made fun of him because he cried for her for so long. Now he finally found a new love, Claire, but deep inside he thinks of Abby. I guess he always will love her and have a sweet spot in his heart for her. Now he's a father and happy and a famous author. I'm so proud of my bro.

I take Paige to Cocky Bull. Every damn woman I fucked was there. I wanted to run but I had to show her that my feelings for her were true. I will move heaven and earth for her. We start to drink, keeping her very close to me. The music is loud. I start kissing her neck and biting her earlobe. She smells divine. She's wearing a short skirt with heels that could poke your eye. She always looks like a sexy secretary. She wears huge black glasses. She's a bit drunk and starts to sing Kelly Clarkson's *Stronger:* "You think you got the best of me; what doesn't kill you makes me stronger." She is dancing and swaying that beautiful ass. She's beautiful. Her blonde hair falls from her bun. She takes her glasses off. My lord, she's sexy as hell. My dick is twitching. A guy grabs her. I'm like a mad dog, getting that dude and beating his ass. I tell Paige, "Let's get out of here; you don't belong in a place like this." All Paige could do is smile. When we got in my car I couldn't wait to touch her sweet spot with my finger. I made her come apart with those sweet sounds, licking her sweet juices. We both grin because she sucks my cock like she has a candy stick.

CHAPTER 17

Emily

It's been months since John walked out on me. My life is getting somewhat normal. The tears finally stopped and the loneness seems less empty. My children call me to see how I am or come to visit when they need me. Life is back to normal. I started running. Taking a deep breath, the smells of the outdoors are amazing. The skies are blue, birds are singing. The sounds are beautiful. My neighbor is always outside smoking a cigar, blinking at me and always showing his beer gut.

Taking a shower, I muse that it's been a while since I felt a man's arms around me. Maybe I was meant to be by myself. Josh tries to call me collect. I never accept his calls. I wish he would just leave me alone. Life is funny; it takes you to a dark place, then the light returns. My life has been dark for so long. The phone rings.

"Hi Paige, how are you? Come over now! I'll be waiting for you; maybe we could watch *Whatever Happened to Baby Jane.* We'll have a couple of beers. You know how much I love classics. Bye sweetie."

Snowball is asleep while Paige and I are talking and watching a movie. "So how are you and Tommy?"

"He asked me to move in with him."

"Really? What I've heard from him is that he never gets close to woman, only if it's sex. What did you tell him?"

"I told him no. I can't go with a guy like that. He's amazing in bed but what happens when he gets tired of me? I can't take that chance."

"It could be he loves you, Paige."

"What I've heard is he never says love or stays for breakfast but with you he's different. What I'm trying to tell you is don't miss out on someone loving you; not all men are the same. We just pick the wrong guys. Oh my God, is she really starving her sister and trying to feed her a dead bird? This movie is awful." We both laugh. I was going to watch *Gone with the Wind* but it's about four hours long. "You're a good friend, Emily."

"So are you."

We keep drinking until Paige leaves. I'm ready for bed when there's a knock. Opening the door it's Wade running in the house.

"I need money, Mom." I give him fifty dollars; he gives me a kiss on the cheek.

"Do you to want to eat?"

"No Mom, got to go pay my friend."

"Are you okay?"

"Don't worry, Mom, I'm fine. Thanks for your help."

"Anytime."

Wade has a family now and he's gambling. He'll be in trouble in no time. He leaves, no matter what age you will always worry about your children.

Rick & Tommy

"I need your help, bro." We're at Denny's eating pancakes.

"Tommy, your appetite is enormous. What's the problem?"

"Well bro, I asked Paige to move in with me."

I splattered all my coffee and started choking; of course, Tommy smirked. "What, bro? Are you all right?"

"I just can't believe what I'm hearing. Tom, you said you would never fall for a woman or love one and that we are dumbasses for falling, like stupid--only a foolish dude falls…"

"Shut up, dumbass. You need to help me, Rick. I'm desperate, bro, please!"

"What do you want me to do, Tommy? If she can't love you then you have to accept it and go on."

"Like you did with Abby?"

"Don't bring her in to this, Tom. She was different. I've loved her since we were six. We reconnected and almost married. Sorry bro, didn't mean to tell you about her. That kind of love only comes once in a lifetime. Tom, if you love Paige, fight with everything you have because you won't get that kind love with another person. When you have a connection like that you want to embrace it with both arms and never let go. I'm very happy but there isn't a day that goes by that I don't think of my angel named Abby."

Tommy is just nodding. Sorry I made fun of you, Rick. It wasn't right; you tried to move on and Betts had an affair with your best friend. You're not going to eat your pancakes?" He takes my plate and eats all my pancakes. Where does it go, Tom you eat like a pig."

"Sweetness, could you bring me some more pancakes and coffee?"

The waitress smiles at him; of course, when the bill is placed on the table on the back is her phone number. Tommy smiles. "See, I'm changing, bro."

Rick just laughs and Tommy throws the receipt in the trash. "Yup, you're in love, Tommy. All I can say is don't let her go or hurt her, because every woman deserves to be loved. Bring her to a barbecue. Claire would love to meet the woman that stole your heart."

Tommy hits Rick's arm. "Come on, dude, be nice."

Sitting and drinking more coffee with Tommy was nice. He's changing and growing up and in love. Love is a precious gift. It could hurt you or make you happy or destroy your heart. A heart is huge. I still love Abby; she's a piece of me and will have a piece of my heart always. I love Claire, my wife, the mother of my children and am very happy. I would never change my life. We spend the day together. We truly miss Scott.

Never a day goes by that we don't think of the loss of our brother.

Emily

I am speaking at a women's group today about my story and how women feel weak because the man makes you feel worthless then they beat you and belittle you and depression sneaks in and this could last for so many years and years, like Josh and me. We were so dysfunctional in our relationship. There was nothing left now. I look back at my life with so many regrets. Josh just wanted to get back at me for hurting Abby, but I was a young girl when I did those things. I'm a good person. He never wanted me, ever, and that hurts so much more. After the group's meeting, all us women are going to a night club to have a few drinks. Maybe some of us will get lucky and get laid, because

BROKEN DREAMS

I'm so horny. Staring at myself in the mirror, my nose is not pretty anymore; it just reminds me what kind of life I had and what I put my children through. My hair is long. I'm wearing a short black skirt with a silk blouse and six-inch black heels. I'm not skinny anymore. What a laugh--I'm curvy in all the right places. Sometimes my arm hurts where Josh broke it. My bones and my right leg are not beautiful prizes anymore. Tears roll softly down my face. My women's group went fantastic. If I could just help one woman, my job is done.

With Paige and two more friends from the safe house, we walk in like we own the place. You know, the look of woman power. We get stares from everyone. We now know we have the power in our minds and body and soul. No one will ever treat us like trash. We all have a seat in a booth. Paige wasn't drinking to drive us home. There were men everywhere and my sweet spot was tingling for someone to touch.

"Would you lovely ladies like a drink?" We all say yes. The guy was a fox, looking like Brad Pitt with a suit.

All of us were just drooling when his friends came over.

"What is this, a handsome men convention?"

The foxy guy asks me to dance. Of course, I say yes. I was getting wet just with him holding my hand. We're dancing slowly. He holds me close; my head presses on his chest. How I miss a man's touch. He takes hold of me tighter. I take a deep breath. He smells divine. He's exactly what I need tonight. We go to the bar.

"What would you like to drink, honey?"

"How about sex on the beach?"

"That could be arranged," he says with a grin.

"What's your name?"

"Emily, and yours?"

Jack stares at me. "You're very attractive, Emily."

"Thanks."

Emily

Paige is dancing; to my surprise it's with Tommy. God, that dude has it bad for her. The way they're dancing, both in love--I want that so badly. Foxy guy asks again if I want to dance. Sure, he only picks slow music.

All my friends are dancing when I turn around in the bar. Trevor is staring at me. Why he can't let me alone? So I kiss Jack. Dear God, he knows how to kiss.

"So when are you going to take me home and have your way with me?"

"When you're good and ready, honey."

"I'm ready now; let me tell my friends."

We're walking out and Trevor stops us. "Where are you going, Em?"

"None of your business, Trevor."

"Don't do this!"

"I'm single; I can do whatever I want."

Jack and I walk out. He has a black Corvette. He takes me to his house in Beverly Hills. He has a beautiful home. Walking inside, he starts to kiss me with so much lust and passion. "Ready to be devoured, honey?" He has me against the wall. I'm so wet and horny. I lick the tip of my finger and pinch my nipple. Jack moans, "You're so naughty, honey." Biting my bottom lip, he starts sucking my tits. Wow! He sucks divine. I can't stop myself making embarrassing sounds. He licks my neck, takes hold of my neck and kisses my mouth roughly; he sticks his finger down to my sweet spot. He carries me to his bedroom. We take our clothes like there was a fire. We were the ones that were so hot and lit up in flames. Jack removes every piece of clothing he was wearing. He is beautiful for a man and his cock is amazingly huge and perfect. "Come here, honey, I'm going to rock your world." I got shy a bit, with all my scars. Jack comes to me. "It's ok, beautiful." My smile was poignant. He starts to kiss me and lays me down. "Open your legs, honey. I love eating bare pussy." He made me come so quick he made my eyes roll back. He lay back. After our shower I sucked his cock clean. He wasn't kidding when he said all night. It was the best night I've had for so long with a man. When I wake up the next morning there's a note telling me it was an amazing night. *Let yourself out. I would like to hire you as my fuck buddy.* Next to the note was five hundred dollars. He thinks I'm a whore. Tears stream down my face. Men are assholes. He made last night dirty. Well, I guess it was kind of nasty. He was a good fuck and I could use the five hundred dollars. I leave with sadness but

content, feeling a need for coffee. I take Snowball for a long walk, thinking of my life. It's windy. The air blows on my face just for a moment. Closing my eyes, I enjoy the breeze. Life is good.

CHAPTER 18

Josh

I wake up in a hospital trying to remember what happened in my cell, then all the memories come to me. One of the inmates tried to kill me. My throat hurts. He sliced my throat. They should've just killed me. I lost so much weigh because of the horrible food. The doctor comes in my room. "You're going to be ok, Josh. You will live."

I close my eyes because truth be told, I don't give a fuck.

"We notified your parents. When you get better

you'll be in protective custody. You will be alone in your own cell. They want to kill you, and we can't have that. Josh, do you know why they would want to kill you?"

All I could do is just shake my head with a loud no. My mind is working in overdrive. All I'm thinking about is Abby. Why? I have no idea. I've always blocked the love I had for her, hiding it way back, festering. My heart is black, with no love. I punished and beat Emily for loving me; now she just hates me and who could blame her? I wanted to kill her for putting me in prison. Maybe with my rage it is where I belonged all long, in a prison for two damn years. I wish was dead; my life is worth shit. Two months later, with a huge scar on my neck, I feel like a freak. Keeping me away from the inmates was the best thing that could've ever happened to me. Abby visited me at night through my dreams, my broken dreams.

I wrote something about my broken dreams:

My dreams are broken. Abby and I have spoken.

She comes with white broken wings into my broken dreams. I'm walking this dirty road; I see a most beautiful angel with a white robe. She has long, dark wavy hair with sadness in her eyes. My heart wants to explode. I just can't erase my memories of her; she's filling my heart and soul. I just can't escape this wonderful nightmare. I don't want to let go or be awakened because she will go away and I will go astray once again. Her arms reach for me but can't reach; that would teach me not to be mean. I don't care, reaching for her again. Please, dear God, let me reach those beautiful hands. She touches my face and her tender hands feel like silk. She doesn't talk; she just holds my face with tears flowing down her cheeks. Her eyes are like glass with a flashing light that hurts my eyes. That's when her warmth fills my heart. She's walking away from me. Don't go, please; don't leave me alone with broken pieces of my broken heart and broken dreams.

BROKEN DREAMS

In my lonely soul the light gets brighter. It hurts my eyes. When I awake, tears sliding down my face, emptiness fills my heart once again. My anger fills my soul and I awake with tears in my eyes.

My days are just counting minutes, hours, days, months… Being in a cell by myself takes a toll on me. I start talking to myself; I know I sound pathetic. I'm just a loser, crying like a sissy. Mom sent me some money and I bought some coffee chips. When you're in prison those are luxuries in this cold, empty place. Dad hasn't talked to me since I told him to take me out of here but he said no. I got sliced on my throat from an asshole that was trying to kill me. If he only knew that I wanted to die he would've done me a favor, that cocksucker. Now I have a huge scar on my neck. All I do is read, sleep and exercise. They cage us like animals; what do they expect from us? I have my own pot so I can make coffee all day if I want. I remember Abby in the market holding a Starbucks. She looked so beautiful. She was happy. She could've been mine. Why did I let her go? It was ignorant in my part. I never got to make love to her. She would've loved me more than those two pricks. I hate the fact they got to touch her and I didn't--what a loss. Abby's kisses were heaven; now I'm stuck in this hellhole for eight more months. As long as Mom sends me money I'll be fine. I can't believe they gave me *The Notebook* to read. I started to read and couldn't put that damn book down. It took me away from my reality. Son of a bitch--who would've thought. I read so much. My time was going quickly so I keep reading all the drama and mystery books. It kept me going and that's all I could ask for. I'm still alive and that's what counts, but I'm a mean son of a bitch.

Tommy & Paige

"Listen sweetheart, you love me; why not be together? I want you, just you, all of you. I won't let you go. I've never told anyone those words. I love you, Paige. I know you had a bad marriage. That won't happen with me, I promise, baby."

Looking in the mirror, I'm rehearsing what I'm going to tell Paige. I thought it sounded sincere because I'm genuinely going to marry that woman. Now I'm going to stop by Tracy's café for my free coffee and muffin before work. She's a babe for still giving me free stuff when she's not with Rick anymore. I feel sorry for the gal; she has two kids. The dude left her and now Tracy has to work harder. She still loves Rick but she made her bed and now she has to lie in it. I don't wish her bad but she did hurt my bro and he would have made her happy.

I bought a house up in the Montecito Heights. The houses are old but the view is to die for. Rick was helping with the fixing and remodeling for when Paige says yes. I put a new fireplace because we will be making some nasty love. She's sexy as hell. New bathrooms--everything is new in the kitchen, even if she doesn't cook for shit. Good thing I know how to make peanut butter, thanks to mommy dearest. I chuckle at myself. The day went quickly, meeting Paige for dinner then taking her to the new house--our new house. I want to make her happy, my lovely beauty.

I went to pick the most beautiful rock that I could afford from Tiffany. That woman is not going to tell me no this time. She's the first woman that I had to fight for. By God, she will say yes. Paige and I are eating she's so beautiful with that navy silk dress. I wanted to fuck her on the table. I adjust my cock to calm down. *All in good time, boy.* She smiles at me. "So how was your day, sweetie?"

"Very nice, Tom. With all those flowers you sent, you actually made my day. Even Emily was happy. It brightened our office."

We smile at each other like teenagers. "Are you ready for your surprise, Paige?"

"Yes, let's go!"

I take her to the new house. "Don't say anything, Paige until I say okay."

She nods. We go inside. All the candles are on; roses are everywhere; the fireplace is on.

"Wow! Tom, this is lovely."

We walk in front of the fireplace. I touch her face. "You're beautiful, honey."

Passionately our lips meet; our sexual desires are boiling to the hottest temperature. In that silk dress I could feel all her curves as my hand traced every inch of her body. "I want to make sweet love to you, Paige."

"Then stop talking and do it; I'm all yours."

Laying her on the floor, pulling her dress off, she

has a beautiful navy lace Demi bra with a matching thong. My cock twitches a couple of times. Wanting to last, I strip my pants off. "You see how my huge cock wants you, baby?"

She smiles. I start to hold my shaft. "Do you want this baby? Answer yes!"

With her low voice, almost like a whisper, I remove my shirt. Her name is on my chest.

"Tom, when did you get that tattoo?"

"I told you, don't say a word." Slowly my tongue goes in her mouth, swirling in her lovely taste of saliva. It was more like devouring with so much passion and lust. My finger goes straight to her sweet spot. She was so soaked it was driving me crazy. I slurp her nipple. The noises that are coming from her sweet mouth are out of this world. I've been with so many women, and none of them come close to this beautiful goddess. I give the other nipple a slurp.

"Tom, it feels so good. Don't! Please don't stop, Tommy!"

I know she's feeling so good; she never calls me Tommy. My inside wanted to decompose. I start to lick her belly button. She massages my head, then I go her to her pussy and open those lips, licking her walls, tasting her lovely essence. My cock can't take it anymore but I hold back. This is her night. We're full of sweat from our anticipation. I go on with the sweet torture; my face digging. My tongue goes deeper and deeper to her pussy.

"Oh! Tommy! Oh my God! I'm coming, baby! I'm coming."

Her yells were driving me insane. She has an intense orgasm. I smile at this goddess in front of me. My cock is more ready for her sweet spot. Sliding in her warm pussy was divine. Lifting her legs on my shoulders, my moves are so slow, back and forth, touching her thighs, pumping more aggressively, pumping more. "Oh yeah! Yeah! Ahhh! That's it honey; that's it." We come in the same moment. We hold each other. "That was amazing, Tom."

"There's more where that came from, sweetheart. Paige, I never knew what love was until I met you. Sure, I went with lots of women but what I feel for you is love, passion, lust and I love you. Paige, would you marry me, because I can't live without you. I want to spend the rest of my life with you. Please don't say no. I will love you forever, I promise." Paige's tears were flowing down her face; she truly loved Tom. "Paige, please say something."

"Yes, Tom! Yes!"

"You're saying yes, honey. God, I love you so much!" He kisses her with so much passion and hunger.

We made sweet love all night long. "I've never been happier in all my life. This is true love. It came late in my life. I will embrace this true love for the rest of my life. By the way, this is our house I bought it for you, honey."

"Oh Tom, I love you so much it hurts--not to make love to you every second of the day, sweetheart; that will never be a problem"

We both laugh. This is happiness. We go at it like jackrabbits once again.

CHAPTER 19

Trevor

I miss Em. I've been going to my AA meetings. I don't want to be the man I used to be. Rick was kind enough to help me after what I did to him, breaking up his marriage to Betty. Well, you can't cry over spilled milk. Betts is gone now; she took her life and we had to go on with our lives without her. She was my friend. I see that Emily got a cute dog she walks every day. She's beautiful. I could watch her every minute of every day. Maybe one day she could love me and maybe my two children could accept me as their father. I've always loved them and now, thinking about it, they do look like me. Josh made their lives miserable and that fills my heart with sadness. If I had known I would've kick Josh's ass for treating my children like that! Piece of shit loser--just to think he was my best friend. We even shared cunts together. If I see him again…it's better not to think about it because truth be told, he's not worth going to jail for. Having dinner just by myself is pathetic. The waitress is just smiling at me. I am horny but I'm not that way anymore. I leave before I get myself in trouble at the market and who do I see but Emily.

"Hi! How are you?"

"Fine Trevor, what are you doing here?"

"Well, I have to eat."

"Yes, you do; sorry."

"That's okay."

"Trevor, I don't mean to be rude."

"Would you like to go have coffee with me?"

"I don't think that will be a good idea."

"Nice seeing you, Em."

"Nice seeing you."

She's walking away. I guess this is for the best. Emily smiles at me. "Why not, Trevor? It's just coffee; that's all, Trevor."

I wanted to jump up and down. We go to Starbucks. Em was wearing jeans and a cute blouse. She always had a lovely body. We laugh and talk for hours, just like old friends. I realized how much I've missed my friend, the mother of my children. I didn't want it to end.

She starts to say goodbye. I kiss her forehead. "Thanks Em, for spending time with me. It meant a lot to me."

"Thank you for the latte, Trevor, and the pastry."

We both have unhappiness. We say goodbye. That was the best time I've had for so long. Life goes on without my Em.

Emily

Seeing Trevor was a surprise. Having coffee with him brought back so many memories. He's so gorgeous. He has so many tattoos now, and he has muscles that any woman wants to touch and lick. What am I thinking? He's not the guy I want to spend the rest of my life with; he is the father of Trina and Travis. They grew up to be wonderful children despite the harsh way Josh treated them. The environment was so dysfunctional; how could I let them go through all that heartache? I could never fix or change any of that. It saddens me so much. It wasn't fair for them. Wade is the one that got the love from his dad and me. Now he's trying to live right but he has that bad boy side, always getting in trouble. I will always worry about that boy. Now he's a handsome man. All my children are beautiful.

Another boring day at home when I get a phone

call from John. He tells me Josh will be getting out of prison in one month. All I tell him is ok; what else could I say? Josh did his time; all I could hope for is he doesn't come and kill me for sending him away. Josh might come out worse than when he went in. I'm going to leave it in God's hands. Snowball wants to take a walk. We start walking. The next-door neighbor is wearing shorts and a tight t-shirt with his gut showing. Sometimes I wonder if he washes those clothes.

"Hi baby, you're looking good."

"Thanks." My cheeks flush; he's so embarrassing.

"Are you blushing, baby cakes?"

I walk faster to get away from him.

"Don't be shy, baby, you're looking good."

Wow! He's relentless. Taking my time walking is my past-time. Breathing the fresh air, my hair blowing on my face, taking deep breaths--I never felt so much freedom in all my life. I went to Tracy's café for coffee and a croissant. We're helping a young girl with three kids. Her husband tried to kill her and not just one time but various times. It saddens me that she's going through all this heartache. For so many years Josh hit and beat me and I let him. So much guilt and shame has always filled my heart, but I grew up and got wise. I will never get beaten up ever; that's what I promise myself. Life goes on alone. I'm okay with that just as long I can breathe my freedom, and that's all that matters.

Rick & Claire

It's Valentine's Day. I'm going to surprise my baby with breakfast in bed. Our kids are at school. Thank God it landed on a weekday. I'm singing in the kitchen, making bacon and eggs, muffins, strawberries and whipped cream and orange juice--and roses, pink roses. We've been so happy, even though I still think of Abby. That woman will always be in my heart. She still holds my heart after what seems like forever. I take the tray in our room. "Baby, wake up. Here's your Valentine's breakfast."

"Wow! Thanks Rick. This is lovely, sweetheart.

"You're the one that's beautiful baby."

She grins like I gave her the world. Maybe for her I did. We eat our breakfast. Claire starts to feel my penis. She sure knows how to arouse my throbbing steel rod. She gifts me by sucking the tip, teasing with little gentle bites that drive me insane. She squeezes my balls. I just wanted to explode. "Come in my mouth," she says, putting whip cream on it and licking it like it's a popsicle. Her sweet moans and groans are amazing to hear. She holds my cock and starts to put it in her mouth once again, inch by inch, until my cock touches her throat. "Almost there, baby," she moans and with that my cum flows inside her throat. I spread her thighs and I lick her vagina until she calls my name. I take her to dinner at Denny's with the kids. We all give Valentine's cards and we go to the park for a while so the kids could play. We're one happy family. I love being a father. I waited so long to be this happy. I would never change my life. I'm so glad my brother Tommy has fallen in love. He was a man whore but now he's so in love with Paige. He bought her a house. I'm very happy for them. I'm taking a shower and Claire comes in and she joins me and we go at it again with our amazing sexcapade--what a beautiful life.

Josh

Reading is my favorite thing to do here at prison. There's nothing else to do here in this god-forsaken cell with the tiniest window. Two more days and I'm out of here—freedom. I can't wait to get some pussy. I'm so horny. It's been two and a half years.

Two days passed slowly but I'm walking out of this awful prison. Dad came to pick me up. He looks old. I guess losing Kyle and having a worthless son will age a person. "Hi dad!"

"How are you, son?"

"Very well considering you didn't help me out."

"Don't start, Josh; you're to blame for your mistakes. Stop blaming us."

"Whatever."

We drive away. He takes me to eat a huge cheeseburger. I devour the sorry-ass cheeseburger. What dad doesn't know is I wanted a slut to fuck her brains out, not this cheeseburger; it is not enough. Staying at Mom and Dad's house is the worst. They're telling me what to do. I get dressed up. "Where are you going?" Dad says.

"I'm going out, Dad. You want me to tell you why? I haven't been with a woman for so long." Dad just nodded his head; what else can he say? Walking in Cocky Bull I could see people's expressions. They're in shock. Yeah assholes, I'm back and looking around for whoever wants to meet my cock. I take a seat. The bartender asks, "What's your pleasure, Josh?"

"Give me two shots and a bud." When I turn around, hearing some woman laughing, fuck, it's Emmy. Wanting to kill her, I just stay put. It's karaoke night. Our eyes connect. She's not scared of me anymore. Good for her, stupid bitch. Emily is going to sing. She looks beautiful but the anger I have toward her… Then she starts to sing *Stronger* by Kelly Clarkson: *What doesn't kill you makes you stronger…* Her voice is wonderful. All the words were for me. *…you tried to break me…* All the ladies were yelling, "You go, girl."

Emily's eyes never left mine. I continue to drink. A woman has a seat next to me. I give her my best grin.

"Hi, I'm Tammy, what's your name?"

"Does it really matter?"

"Not really, I just want a good time."

"Well let's go to your place."

"Ready when you are."

This woman is hot! Tight jeans with very high

heels with a blouse that falls off her shoulders, black long wavy hair, full red lips, chocolate brown eyes-- just beautiful. My cock wants to burst. Tammy's house is small but comfy. Taking off my jacket, she smiles. "Let's go to my room." We walk in. Her room has a fireplace. I don't waste any time, not having a woman for two and a half years. We start to kiss, our tongues dancing a unique rhythm. She has a tongue ring. I can't wait until she uses that metal tongue piercing on my cock. I grab her roughly. "Sorry baby, I like to fuck hard."

"Then fuck me rough." Having her on the edge of the bed, my cock slips in hard. She screams with pleasure. Banging her in and out felt amazing. When our sexcapade was over we slept in each other's arms. When I woke up she surprised me with her tongue on my penis. With that tongue ring it was a sensation of pure ecstasy. I started to crash at her house almost every day.

CHAPTER 20

Josh

My life wasn't worth living. My life was spiraling out of control. Tammy was a drug dealer who gave me drugs every day. She kept asking me if I wanted heroin. Finally I gave in. We had orgies; we had unrestrained sexual activity; we indulged in wild sex and drinking parties. Every day was a different partner. I didn't care about anything anymore. I would be sleeping and the woman would lick my cock, then she would sit on top and fuck me like she was riding a horse. I was a pitiful mess and with all I've done I had no regrets—well, maybe just one: leaving Abby. She was the only love in my life. Marrying Emily was my mistake. I hated her, the damn bitch. We're all drinking again. I no longer step outside. I'm living like a junkie with different women all day every day. Doing heroin you feel like all your dreams will come true. It takes control of your life. Having more sex and drugs, I lost more weight. My life is like a roller coaster. Tammy makes sure I don't withdraw, so she keeps the supply coming. I'm starting to get awful marks on my arm. I don't eat much. Some bitch is coming my way. "Go get a beer."

She smirks at me but at least she brings it to me. "And get away from me; my cock is tired of you bitches." Walking to the restroom to vomit, I feel sick. I don't know if I need more drugs or I took too much.

Tammy walks in. "What's wrong, sugar?"

"I don't feel too good."

"I'll fix you up, sugar" She helps me to the bedroom. She starts to prepare a needle and she injects my arm. My eyes roll back into my head. She starts to kiss me; our tongues dance to the rhythm and with the drugs flowing through my veins we get it on. She lets me do whatever; she kind of reminded me of Betty. She knows I love fucking her ass. I'm slapping her incredible ass hard and my iron steel rod stands straight. I bang her sweet ass to kingdom come. Waking up was the worst because all I wanted was drugs; that's all my body was asking for, more and more drugs that were controlling my pitiful life.

Trevor

When I saw Josh he seemed worse than when he went to prison. I hope he gets his act together and he's with a beautiful woman who deals drugs. I wish I could help my once-best friend. Now we're just enemies. Very disturbing, the way he looked. I still care about him. If there is anything I've learned it is that you have to help yourself before you help someone else.

Emily

Seeing Josh was a shock. He looked like he always looked, mean with a cold soul. At first I really thought he wanted to kill me but he thought it best to leave me alone, thank goodness. I was tossing and turning. I couldn't sleep. I was feeling the storm is coming. Feeling uneasy, I'm looking at myself in the mirror. Something is going to happen. Tears are sliding slowly down my face when I hear a knock. I run to the door. It was Josh. He looked like death. Josh falls on my front porch.

"What happened, Josh? Let me call the paramedics."

"Don't Em, it's too late. I need to tell you

something."

I hold him tight on my chest. "Please don't die, Josh, please! "

"Em, I'm so sorry for the way I treated you. All I wanted all my life is to go with Kyle."

My tears are flowing. I'm crying a river. "You're going to be ok, Josh."

He stared coughing badly. "Tell Wade I love him." Tears were flowing down his face.

"Let me call for help, Josh."

"NO!" I stayed with Josh and kissed his forehead, our tears flowing. "Tell Abby I always loved her. It was always her, Em."

"Whatever you say, Josh."

"Promise me!"

"I promise."

Sorry for what I did to you." Then he took his last breath.

I'm yelling, "No, don't go, please Josh!"

The man next door comes up, half-nude. "What's

wrong, baby cakes?"

I roll my eyes. "Call for help, please."

"Well, little lady, he looks dead."

"Call for help!"

He turns and runs, falling on his stomach, to go get help with his butt cheeks all for the world to see. He was wearing women's underwear. I wanted to weep and laugh at the same time.

Josh passed away. I was weeping all night. Being by myself was the best because I just wanted to be alone. I fell asleep hours later. My pillow was soaked with tears. He gave me the worst life ever but I loved him then. Years passed; he was horrible to me, then more years passed and it worsened. My heart is broken; with his passing my broken dreams went with him.

Trevor wakes me up. My face must've looked swollen. He put his arms out and I embrace them with so much sadness. "It's okay, baby girl, Josh is where he wants to be--with his brother in heaven."

Sobbing is all I could do; there is nothing else to do but weep for a life lost.

Emily & Trevor

Telling my children what happened and telling Josh's mom and dad was very awful. I wish could take the pain for them but that was impossible. They are great parents; now they have to bury another son. I ask them if they need help with funeral arrangements. They said they will do it themselves and Debbie would help. His sister took it hard.

Trevor went to work and I was grateful; he was hovering over me. The phone rings.

"Hello, it's John. Sorry to hear Josh passed away."

"Thanks John, it's very kind of you to care about me."

"Yes, I do care, Emily." I roll eyes. I don't want to

do this right now. "But you let Trevor in."

"I didn't let anyone in; he came because he cares about me."

"I'm going to pick you up for the funeral, Emily."

"Why John? We're not together anymore."

"As friends; we are still friends, Emily."

"Whatever; do what you want, John." I hang up. I can't deal with this right now. Wade cried for hours, saying, "Why Mom, why?"

All I could say is that he's in a better place. Life has loss, love, and disappointments. We have to go on and this is the honest truth.

After a few days I was still in bed drinking some wine and feeling all my regrets. My emotions were all over the place. I was feeling sorry for myself and drunk; talking to myself and laughing, opening another bottle of wine.

Trevor walks in.

"What do you want?"

"Your drunk and tomorrow is the service."

"So what!? Just leave me on my own. You don't belong here; you're just as messed up as Josh."

"Don't compare me to Josh. I never treated you badly. I always loved you."

"Stop saying that."

"You're sad right now because deep down you always loved Josh, but guess what? He never loved you."

Tears streamed down my face. "Get out! I hate you!"

"You don't hate anyone, baby girl; you're a kind and beautiful loving woman, so stop! Let me take care of you." She puts her wine glass on the table and walks to her bed. Trevor helps her with her pajamas, fixing her pillows and gently wraps her blankets around her. He watches her sleep.

I love her and want her so badly but she'll never want me. I could make her happy. I want to make her blissfully happy. What could I possibly do to make her love me? I ask myself. At some point falling into a deep sleep holding her was the best night ever; unfortunately, it's just one night but I'll take what I could get. All I want is Emily.

When she woke up she had a hangover and her eyes were swollen. She's a strong woman. I wish she could marry me and live the end of our lives in a huge bubble of delightful bliss. Man, that's been my dream since the day I made love to her. We were young and we made foolish decisions and lots of broken dreams. Wretchedness filled my soul and my heart. We all were broken.

Rick & Tommy

Tommy came to my house to tell me the terrible news that Josh has passed away. I wasn't surprised because of the life he was living and the kind of drugs he was taking. It really saddened me.

"Tommy, are you going to the services?"

"Yes! Are you?"

"Yes! I should. I didn't like him but I feel sorry for Emily. She suffered at the hands of Josh; it's just horrific what he made his kids through. Hey bro, do you think Abby will be there?"

"I don't think Tyler will let her. He protects her from all this drama, and who could blame him?"

"I wish I could see her for the last time. What am I saying? That woman has a hold of heart to this day."

Tommy is watching my struggles. "You still love her, Rick?"

"I will always love that girl. I do love my life with Claire. I couldn't ask for a better woman."

Tommy doesn't say a damn thing because he will never feel that because he would never compromise his relationship. He loves Paige and always will and she loves him too! Abby didn't love Rick like that; she loved him as a friend. My bro and I go and buy a suit and some shoes. We spend the day together. We're no longer taking anything for granted. We lost Scott but we still have each other. "Look bro, we still got all these women staring at us."

I roll my eyes. "So what? We're in love, remember? Let's go have coffee at my favorite place, Tracy's café."

"Sure, wherever you want."

Tommy is like a kid going to a candy store. Tracy is always cheerless. It makes me mad that Rex up and left her. Tommy rushes to say "Hi Tracy!"

"Hi Tom, the usual?"

"Sure, is it for free?"

She laughs. "Yes Tom, always free for my best customer."

He smiles of course. Nodding my head was the norm when I'm with Tommy. "Hello Tracy."

"Hi! Rick, you're looking good like always"

"And you're still beautiful, I see. "

"Thanks Rick. What would you like?"

"Let me have same as Tom."

We both smile and Tommy and I take seats. "She's still into you, Rick!"

"Please eat your muffin and shut up!"

"Ok bro, whatever you say."

Then he started with he's jokes. He had me choking on my coffee. I love my brother. I would never change the way he is, so full of life and love inside his beautiful heart. We say our goodbye to Tracy and go our merry way.

CHAPTER 21

Josh's Funeral Service

T ommy and I go to have a seat. Claire stayed with the kids at home. Emily is sobbing. All her children were here with the exceptions of Travis and Trina. Wade is the one who was crying so badly. Sorrow surrounded this whole room in the church of God. The casket was closed. Thank God; we didn't need to see him in the end of his life. Everyone was taking a seat. It was so silent you could hear a pin drop. Travis comes with Josh's parents. It was heartbreaking to say the least. The pastor begins when Tommy kicks my leg and whispers, "She's here."

"Who's here?" I turn and my stomach felt the butterflies fluttering. She's the most beautiful woman I've ever seen, with a black fitted dress with six-inch heels, her dark long hair, her fair skin, red full lips; her long lashes made her eyes sparkle. She sees me and she gives me her stunning shy smile, and I actually blush-yeah, me blush. I wanted to run to her but Tyler took her way on the other side of the room. I was mesmerized by her.

Tommy whispers in my ear. "I know this is epic but you're staring, Rick. Tyler is noticing."

I turn quickly. We listen to the pastor. Everyone was sobbing. They asked Emily to say something; she said no. Trevor said a few words.

"I don't know how to feel about Josh. He gave Emily a miserable life; her face is not the same because he broke her nose so many times." His parents were weeping, then Abby, with her head up high, walks to Emily and she opens her arms to her. Emily hugs her tightly. They're talking and Abby wipes her tears away. I couldn't stop watching her. She hugs his parents. The service was over. We all walked outside.

Tyler tries to take Abby. She tells him something. He nods. She walks toward me and my smile is nervous. The way she sways toward me with so much confidence as she gives me her hand, I cannot resist. I kiss her palm. She has tears in her eyes and I hold her to me. She weeps in my chest and I begin to shed tears with her, tears of love, friendship and the passion we once had. I feel her close to me; she's whispering, "I will always love you, Rick!"

Abby stares in my eyes. We smile. I kiss her on the cheek. "Tyler is waiting for you," I whisper in her ear.

She nods her head. "I've always loved you, Rick."

She turns and walks out of my life forever.

Tyler says goodbye and life goes on without the one woman I can't ever have. If she only knew she was weeping on my chest where I have her tattoo--such a beautiful angel. I never thought I would see her again but life has a funny way of bringing such dreams and hopes and special loves back to your life when you don't expect it.

We all go to Josh's parents' house. His picture is there with Kyle when they were young, beautiful boys. I start to talk to Emily about fixing her nose and I asked her if I could write her story, *Broken Dreams*. She hugs me.

"Thank you so much, Rick.

"You could keep all the royalties from *Broken Dreams* as my gift to you, Emily."

Emily tells me that Josh always loved Abby. He hated her because she was the mean girl and treated Abby awful.

"Let it go, Emily; you've gone through so much. It's time to be happy."

Emily thanks me again. "Rick, you're truly an awesome guy."

I hug her and give her a kiss on her forehead when

John walks in and Trevor's face saddens. He loves Emily but I really don't think he's good enough for her. She deserves a man that will love her every minute of every day. Tommy is eating all the platters. It's amazing how he could eat and not gain an ounce.

"Will you leave some for the other people that are probably hungry?"

"Come on, Rick, people want to drink, not eat." I shake my head.

We stay a while and I'm watching Trevor staring at Emily and John. He's talking to her and holding her hand. They both love her; too bad she has to be alone when she's grieving. I can't say I feel bad Josh is gone because he gave more heartache than love. Trevor starts to smoke a cigarette.

"What's up, you? When did you start to smoke?"

"Yeah, the cravings are driving me crazy. Rick."

"Then you need to go to an AA meeting."

"Just seeing Emily, it breaks my heart that I can't hold or console her."

"Just let her be for now; you can't force someone to love you--I should know!"

"Abby loves you; look at the way she hugged you at the church, tears falling on your chest." Tyler's face was priceless.

"It wasn't like that. She was just saying goodbye forever. We had a special love once; now it's friendship."

We stare at each other like we both know it's true; it's over and life goes on and with that comes love, sadness, kindness and mistakes.

Emily

I woke up the next day empty but refreshed. John is coming to talk. He wants to talk to me about something. I don't know what he wants to talk about; he left me for being unfaithful. I take a shower and put my jeans on with a black sweater, some black boots and my long hair in a ponytail, with light make-up. There's a knock at the door and I take a deep breath. When I open the door it's Trevor. "What are you doing here?" This is all I needed, having both them here fighting.

John is wanting to come back with me because he forgives me; why can't life be easy for me? "Well answer me."

"I need to talk to you and this is my only chance, baby girl."

"John is coming over; if he finds you here…"

"Let me tell you what I need to tell you."

"Okay, tell me. Emily, I can't live without you anymore. I would do anything for you to love me. No one will ever love you the way I've always loved you, so please Emily, you're my heart; you've always been the one. Let me in your heart so I could show you."

There's the knock. My nerves are all over the place at what Trevor just said. Opening the door, John is standing there all handsome with a black suit. "Well, I thought we would be alone." Trevor speaks up. "I'm here to tell Emily that I want to spend the rest of my life with her."

"Are you considering his proposal?"

"I'm not considering anything! Why are you here. John?"

"I wanted you back, Emily. I don't want to live without you, sweetheart."

My tears are smoothing down my cheeks. "I won't choose. I love you both but I'd rather stay alone than choose; I'm so sorry."

They stay speechless until Trevor says, "Then love both of us."

"Are you crazy?"

"Think about it, Emily; you have two men madly in love with you. We would cherish you every day and love you all the time."

"I don't share," John says.

"Would you rather not live with Emily or be in her life?"

John pulls his hair back, thinking what to do next. "This is crazy; we can't all live in the same house."

Trevor says, "I'm in. I would do anything for Emily if she could love us both. Why not both of us loving her at the same time?"

Emily is starting to think. "Could I love both at the same time, and in bed?"

"Stop thinking, baby; if John says no you still have me. I will love you always; you have me, baby girl." My heart was beating hard; my stomach felt all the butterflies fluttering.

"It sounds so erotic; what would my children say?" My thoughts were all over the place. "Could you both leave? I need to think."

Emily

I was watching porn to see how they had a threesome. It scares me to know that two men could be inside me at the same time, and yet I'm I considering two gorgeous men to spend the rest of my life with. I always knew I had a naughty side; why not explore more? Watching the two guys filling her every whim was so erotic, drinking my wine and feeling sexually aroused with no man in sight. I spread my legs. My fingers slip down my pussy, rubbing my sweet spot. The feeling was splendid since I haven't had a man for a while. I licked my fingers and pinched my nipples. Hmm! It really had an effect on my wet pussy; all I could do was squirm on the sofa and my intense orgasm subsides. My peaceful sleep comes with serene dreams. I sleep for more than eight hours. It felt so good to sleep like; it's that been so long. Rick is taking me to the hospital so I could have surgery on my nose. Claire took care of me; she's very nice; she didn't let anyone know. I was there. It made me think, what was I going to do about John and Trevor? Weeks passed. I was feeling awesome. My nose looked beautiful. I felt like a new woman, and free. Claire and I go shopping. We are close friends now. I always wanted a friend. I couldn't trust Betts; she slept with Josh and Trevor and we ended our friendship, then she died. All our lives were not so good and yet we survived the pain and sorrow of life's tragedies and loss. Life is tough. We make all our mistakes but we have to go forward and try to live life the best we can. With so much loss in the past few years I want to live again, to be free from my past life, to be happy for once. That's all I could hope for at this chapter of my life. Still feeling the loss of Josh, trying to go on with my life, more days passed. It was getting easier to bear. All I could think of is being happy. Looking outside, the sunlight was beautiful. With my thoughts praying to God that my life could get easier I saw Abby. She is a special person. Hugging me, I told her that Josh always loved her. Tears were streaming from both our faces; she just said she was sorry and I told her the same. We held each other tightly and with that went our aggression of the past and all was forgiven.

CHAPTER 22

Emily & Trevor

Two months pass. I'm having dinner with both men. I can't wait, licking my lips with so much anticipation. My body tingles just thinking about them. John doesn't like Trevor, so I don't know how this will work with us living together. I'm wearing a tight fitted red dress and have been working out. I have on six-inch red heels; my hair is straight. I told them I'd just meet them at the restaurant; they agreed. Walking in the restaurant, John and Trevor stand up from their seats.

BROKEN DREAMS

My smile is filled with so much gratitude and love swaying my body. Their smiles are lovely. I have a seat staring at John with a suit and Trevor with nice shirt and black slacks. I have a seat facing them. John speaks first. "I won't be joining your threesome. With a distressed face he stares straight in my eyes. "Sorry Emily, I can't share you. "If," he pauses, "I can't have you for myself," he swallows, "I'd rather be alone. Let Trevor love you; he's a good man when not whoring around." He holds my hand. "I love you, Emily, and I always will."

Trevor stays quiet and holds my other hand. Sadness fills my heart; who could blame him? It was a crazy idea. I can't believe I was considering it. Everything in my life has always been complicated.

"That's okay; I will respect your decision. I have to accept the punches of life. I've always have and always will. John, could you join us for dinner before you leave?"

He smiles. "Of course, Emily."

We drink wine, we talk about work, we share our meals like everything is all right, like friends. It felt awesome that we could be friends, and that melts my heart. I enjoy another glass of wine. I haven't been this happy for so long. Trevor looks delicious and well, John is sexy as hell. I better stop looking at porn; it's getting me hot and bothered. Sadness sinks in my heart because all good things come to an end. John kisses my lips with so much yearning. He made his choice and I respect him. He leaves. Trevor smiles at me. "Well, I guess I'll walk you to your car, beautiful."

"Thanks, Trevor, for everything."

"It's my pleasure, baby girl."

Trevor and I walk to my car. He gives me a peck on my cheek. Well, I was not having that. I grab his face and give him a delicious, wet kiss. He moans. We're messing around like two horny teenagers. His fingers hold my neck firmly; he kisses me with so much lust and longing I couldn't breathe and I didn't care. I wanted wild, passionate sex and kisses. He was pressing his bulge; he was getting huge. He started to feel my breasts and my hand was holding his large cock. I was so hot and wet. I didn't want to wait. I wanted him now but he stops. "Let's go because I'm going to fuck you on top of the car for everyone to see, so let's go because I'm going to fuck you good and hard."

When he says those nasty words, I get wetter. "We better hurry because I'm going to burst like right here, right now."

We're going kind of fast, hoping we don't get a ticket. Trevor's hand is under my dress touching my sweet spot; his fingers are inside my pussy. "Oh! Yeah baby."

He removes his fingers and all I could do is pout. "Don't stop!" Staring up at him, he is licking his fingers. "That was so hot. You want a taste of dessert?" He put one finger into my mouth; the taste of salty essence was driving me crazy and so erotic. I was so aroused with all that teasing Trevor was doing. He opens my car door and carries me inside the house. He throws me on the bed. This is a side I never seen of Trevor; he's always gentle, but I love this beautiful man. The roughness in a good way and him teasing me makes me want him even more. All I could do is giggle. Trevor stares at me, loving the fact he seems so happy that I'm the one making him happy.

He loved her giggles; the sound was like heaven. This is Emily; the one I fell madly in love with. "You want me, baby girl?" Holding my cock, still giggling. I'm going to take your clothes off with my teeth. I put music on. The song plays *Staying Alive* from the Bee Gees. Emily couldn't stop laughing. Trevor is dancing like a stripper, taking clothes off piece by piece.

I was shaking my hips; her eyes were open wide. It was so comical. Her face was full of desire, I want her every inch of her skin, her love--everything she wants. Once my clothes came off I was still dancing for her; she was giggling like a beautiful woman should.

"Ready for me, baby girl?"

"Stop teasing me, Trevor; I want you all of you every minute of every day."

I stop dancing. "Are you sure, Emily, because I can't live without you baby, I just can't."

We both were silent for a few seconds. She opens her arms. "Come to me, Trevor. I love you and always will. Make love to me."

We made love all night.

Waking up with the love of my life was incredible. I waited all my life for Emily and I won't let her go, ever. She was satisfied and sound asleep. She's so beautiful. Our life is going to be remarkable. John was a fool not to want her. Well, she's mine now. I make her breakfast in bed. She awakes with a smile. "You're spoiling me."

"Get used to it, baby girl; this will be for the rest of our lives."

"Let's go to the park or the beach; wherever you heart desires."

Trevor and I go to the beach. We hold hands. Life is so much better for both of us. I could feel the tingle in my sweet spot and the warmness in my heart. I'm in love with this gorgeous man who loves me back, but I love John too and my heart hurts for him. Life isn't fair. Trevor turns to me and gives me a kiss to die for. His long tongue makes me want to take my clothes off in front of everyone. He makes me hot. It's a feeling I desired for such a long time, but there is something missing, but I'll take what I could get. Every chance Trevor is squeezing my breast. He like teasing me, touching parts of my body that have me yearning for his delicious tongue and fingers and later his thick penis that I will devour and lick and gently bite with my teeth. Just thinking about is making me so sweltering and drenched. The past days have been heaven. Trevor wants me all the time. He makes feel so beautiful. I'm finally happy and couldn't ask more of my life. We both make dinner. He plays with Snowball. We're so blissful. We go back to work. We're texting each other and we can't wait to see one another. It's so surreal. I feel I'm in a beautiful dream that I never want to wake up from.

EPILOGUE

Trevor and I got married a couple of months later and for my honeymoon we went to Hawaii. He was giving me a gift. Waiting for him on the bed with white lace lingerie with my hair still in a bun with my fluffy slip-on shoes, I was waiting with such eagerness like a good wife. Two men walk out toward me. I was confused. It was John and Trevor in the nude.

"Don't ask any questions, baby girl, just enjoy two men who are over heels in love with you. We want to show you how we could fulfill your every whim and dream."

I was scared. Could I take two men? Well, I'm going to find out because they're coming to me. My body was excited and shaking.

With a whisper John put his finger on my mouth. "Shah! Honey, relish the sensation." He removes my bun from my hair. It flows down. He looks straight into my chocolate eyes. He kisses with such longing. I get on my knees. Trevor comes from behind, giving me sweet kisses on my neck. I start to moan while John is sucking my pink nipples; the sensation was out of this world. He removes my lace lingerie. Trevor licks his finger and he enters his finger in my ass. At first it was uncomfortable but once inside the feeling was overwhelming; meanwhile John was giving me all the attention from the front. I was groaning, "Please! Ahhhh!"

"You're okay, baby girl; let us love you. Can you feel my cock? It wants you so badly."

On my knees I start to lick John's cock. "Oh! Yeah! Baby, suck it hard, yeah! Ahhh! Baby, you're rocking that cock" while Trevor is licking my back side. "Hmmm! Yes, don't stop. Hmmm! Trevor, John, please!"

"What do you need, baby doll? Tell me what you want."

"I want both of you, please."

John looks up to Trevor. John lies down. I'm on top looking at him while my backside is toward Trevor. "Do you feel both of our hearts pumping and our cocks throbbing?"

He slips in my pussy while Trevor enters my backside. I was filled with both cocks, and that feeling was amazing. John is sucking my breast, holding my waist and moving down They both are fulfilling my every need. Trevor gently pushes his cock back and forth. We all came at the same time. It was beautiful and intense, two wonderful men loving me--who would have thought the girl no one wanted was now a woman with two men to love her? Life could bring such enjoyment and sorrow. I was that woman who had dreams and with the wrong guy my dreams were broken. Now I have the wings to fly up to the sky and go outside and yell, "I'm finally happy. Thank you God; I'm not broken anymore."

I have two men living with me and I told my children. They just said they wanted me to be happy. We were all a happy family. Sometimes I think of Josh; he was the love of my life and how our life spiraled out of control with our dysfunctional relationship. He never loved me for being mean to Abby. It all started with Abby and ended with me. What I learned is you can't change or make any man love you. Josh beat me and that wasn't right; what I didn't know was I always had the power and I didn't know! My life was awful once. I'm in love. I work and have my home and two exquisite men who love me and only me. All my five children are doing great. Wade is still struggling; I help him when I can. We're good friends with Rick and Claire and Tommy and Paige. We all get together for BBQs. My dad passed away and my mom is dating now; she's doing lots better. I still work as a counselor for battered women. I will always help women in need. Life is funny; we started with Abby, and now I know that Abby is a great person. I wish the best for her. I was young when I bullied her; that's why no one should be mean to anyone. Karma's a bitch. To all women, you have the power over your life; never let anyone tell you otherwise. You have to love yourself before you can love anyone else. There is always a lesson to be learned. It took me a lifetime but it's never too late. Don't be a life lost; get help or if you know someone is in trouble don't turn away; this could be you. This is the way I felt when I was down.

I have a good side, a bad side, a funny side and a wild side. I live in the dark side of my mind; I stay in the dark most of the time. I don't know why. Maybe I feel safe there. Sometimes I feel like running for dear life but something always stops me and brings me out of the darkness into the light.

I told everyone my story. All the college students

stand up and applaud. If I could help just one person, my job is done. Rick's book *Broken Dreams* made it to number one. I was grateful. It helped with my healing. Life is good and I go home with my two gorgeous men, the loves of my life.

Broken Pieces with a Broken Heart with Broken Dreams

Her heart was broken in so many pieces. She was tired of sobbing and feeling weak. Not wanting to seem like a freak, all she ever wanted was to sneak out to the park, to be free, to breathe the air and feel the wind blowing through her hair; for that young girl that was freedom. She runs smiling for what seems forever in her own kingdom, happy and vivacious, with so much love in her broken heart. She's stronger than she could imagine and time will heal the pieces of her broken heart. That's all she could ask for because truth be told, that's all she ever wanted was to be free and left alone. She watches the trees and the blue sky; she takes deep breaths and closes her eyes. The wind is blowing through her beautiful face. This was all the freedom she could ever desire in her lovely kingdom that's her so-called life. At least she could pretend to be free.

By Martha Perez

A special friend wrote this poem for me...

As children they meet, both trying find hope and Shelter from the abuse--a way to live, to cope. Their friendship is a salve, a Band-aid for their hearts, but time and circumstance bring change, breaking them apart. A chance meeting as adults and sparks turn back into flames. Are they really soul mates or a twist in life's game?

By Cindy J. Smith

Thank you, Cindy!

What doesn't kill you will make you stronger; for sure you are no longer broken or weak because you're stronger than you think. Take a deep breath and in a blink of an eye life goes by. All the pain and suffering certainly made you stronger, so you no longer feel vulnerable. You're definitely, positively stronger. No more sad tears flowing down your cheeks; they're replaced with happy tears, so my dear you made it through your life. Nothing could kill you because living only made you stronger.

Martha Perez

ALSO BY MARTHA PEREZ

Broken Pieces

From a broken home, a dysfunctional family and physical and emotional abuse, Abby finds herself in a bad marriage with two sons. It seems like she'll never escape from the cycle of violence and degradation she's been stuck in for as long as she can remember. But with strength of will and determination, she makes a place in the world for herself. All that's missing is a man to share it with — and then two come along, bringing with them ghosts from her past and forcing her to make a decision on which all her future happiness depends. What will she choose, and will her choice be the right one?

Broken Pieces is a gripping dramatic novel. It tells the story of Abby Marie Pena as she struggles to overcome the hardship and abuse of her difficult childhood to make a way for herself in the world and achieve the happiness she so richly deserves. A strong, resilient woman with boundless reserves of love and compassion, Emily lightens the lives of all those whose paths she crosses and will appeal to a great many readers, male and female, for her moral integrity and awesome courage in the face of seemingly insurmountable obstacles.

Broken Pieces will appeal to those who enjoy dramatic fiction that doesn't sugar-coat the reality of everyday life. Written in a gritty, straightforward style that nevertheless recognizes the potential for love and compassion to illuminate our lives, this is a novel that will live with you for a long time after you have finished.

Broken Heart

What is the nature of true love? How far must we go to vanquish our demons? Is happiness possible? *Broken Heart* will appeal to readers with a passion for drama and romance.

From the esteemed author of the heart-wrenching novel *Broken Pieces* comes the next installment in the same series: *Broken Heart*. *Broken Heart* picks up the story of Rick Owen, following him through the euphoric heights and plummeting depths of his life's struggle with sex addiction and alcoholism. Losing Abby, his brother Scott, and his ex-wife Betty Cox all in one year, he faces a seemingly insurmountable challenge, but with courage and determination he battles on. Will happiness continue to elude Rick, or will he find it in the end? *Broken Heart* will appeal to readers with a passion for drama and romance, and those who enjoy fiction filled with vivid and engaging characters and suspenseful plots.

Martha Perez was born and raised in Los Angeles, CA. She now lives in West Covina, CA with her husband Sal Andalon and their dog Sugar Bear. She is a high school graduate and has a son, a daughter and two granddaughters. Her hobbies include reading, writing, exercise and long walks. *Broken Pieces* is her first book and is an accomplishment of which she is very proud.